THE SOUL TRADE

Also by E. E. Richardson:

The Devil's Footsteps

The Intruders

The Summoning

E. E. RICHARDSON

THE SOUL TRADE

CORGI BOOKS

In association with The Bodley Head

THE SOUL TRADE
A CORGI BOOK 978 0 552 55389 6

First published in Great Britain by Corgi,
an imprint of Random House Children's Books
A Random House Group Company

This edition published 2009

1 3 5 7 9 10 8 6 4 2

The Random House Group Limited supports the Forest Stewardship Council (FSC),
the leading international forest certification organization. All our titles that are printed
on Greenpeace-approved FSC-certified paper carry the FSC logo. Our paper
procurement policy can be found at www.rbooks.co.uk/environment.

Set in 13/17pt Baskerville MT by
Falcon Oast Graphic Art Ltd.

Corgi Books are published by Random House Children's Books,
61–63 Uxbridge Road, London W5 5SA

www.**kids**at**randomhouse**.co.uk
www.**rbooks**.co.uk

Addresses for companies within The Random House Group Limited can be found at:
www.randomhouse.co.uk/offices.htm

THE RANDOM HOUSE GROUP Limited Reg. No. 954009

A CIP catalogue record for this book is available from the British Library.

Printed in the UK by CPI Bookmarque, Croydon, CR0 4TD

For my mother

It was getting late, it was getting dark, and Nick was running out of options. He pulled out his mobile phone and called the only person who might save him.

'Katie! Help!' he said as soon as she picked up. 'I've got to get a present for my stepmum in the next twenty minutes, or I'm toast.' He backed into the shadows of the Westfield Centre shopping mall, trying to keep out of the stream of people leaving through the double doors.

There was a moment's pause. 'Yeah, hello to you too,' Katie said dryly. 'What's going on?'

1

'It's Julie's birthday tomorrow,' Nick explained. 'I've got to get her something, and I have *no* clue what.' He'd planned to start looking last week but the days had slipped away from him. Then Kyle's karate tournament had eaten into Saturday, and this morning his dad had wanted Nick to go and see a film with him . . . 'Seriously, any suggestion would be good right now.' He looked up and down the street but couldn't see a single shop that was even worth stepping into.

'Can't you just give her a card?' Katie sounded distinctly exasperated, but Nick still relaxed a fraction now he had her on the phone. He'd known Katie McManus since playschool, and even then she'd been more organized than he was. He threw himself on her mercy.

'I can't! It was my stepdad's birthday last month and I got him this set of books he'd been trying to find for years. They're out of print and there were only about two places on the internet even selling them . . . I've got to do better than a card.' He held the phone in place with his shoulder as he checked his watch.

There was a brief but loaded pause. 'You're

worried about your step-parents comparing notes?' Katie asked incredulously.

'Well . . . yeah. I mean, Julie knows what I got James.' Nick turned round and pushed through the glass doors into the mall. The crowds had died down to just a trickle of people, and there was a definite feel of things winding down for the day. As he stepped onto the escalators, he could see that several of the smaller shops had already wound down their shutters.

'Did your parents, like, miss a class on how to be divorced or something?' Katie wondered. 'My mum hasn't spoken to my dad for years. And when she does, there's screaming.'

'They just like to make my life difficult,' Nick said.

His parents had split up when he was a baby, but had opted to live close to each other so Nick could still see both of them. Now they'd remarried and had more kids, they tried so hard to make sure Nick spent time with each family that they'd practically merged into a double-sized one – complete with double the hassle. Trying to spend an equal amount of time and effort on everybody, he barely seemed to have a second to himself.

'Come on, Katie, give me an idea here,' he pleaded. 'What's a good stepmum present? The shops are going to close in a minute.' He watched the lights go out in the novelty-candle place as the owner locked up for the night.

'Well, serves you right for leaving it till this late on a Sunday,' Katie chided. 'Give it up and buy her a box of chocolates.'

'She's allergic to nuts. I don't dare.' Nick completed his half-hearted circuit of the upper floor, then swung back towards the down escalator. 'And she doesn't like flowers either. She says they're for dead people.'

'A woman after my own heart,' Katie approved. 'Buy her a cactus.'

For a moment he seriously considered it. 'But . . . don't you think that's sending the wrong message?'

Her sigh crackled in his ear. 'Look, Nicky, at this stage, the only message you've got to worry about is, "Whoops, sorry, I forgot your birthday." Just buy something! *It's the thought* and all that crap. She'll pretend she likes it. She's got manners. Draw her a picture, even! You could give her one of your sketches.'

'I can't do that.' Nick was proud of his artistic ability, but even so. 'That's totally cheap. I wouldn't even have time to do one specially. What am I going to say? "Here, have this page from my sketchbook, I spent two seconds ripping it out just for you"?'

'You make all your own problems, you know that?' Katie huffed. 'Just go into a gift shop, buy the first thing you see that she won't actively hate and go home. OK?'

'Yeah.' Nick had to admit, he probably wasn't going to do any better than that. 'Yeah, I guess I'm going to have to.'

'See? Sorted. And while we're on the subject of birthdays, don't forget it's Daz's bash on Wednesday. You promised you'd come with me, so don't think you're getting out of it.'

'I haven't forgotten,' he said, rolling his eyes. 'I wrote it down and everything, I swear.'

He had to write things down. His parents were both so determined to schedule quality time with him that if he relied on memory he wouldn't know which house he was meant to be in half the time.

'It'll be cool,' Katie said. 'Trust me. You'll have fun.

His parents are going to be away for the night so we've got the whole house to ourselves.'

'I'll be there,' Nick promised, with a faint sigh. Katie had apparently appointed herself in charge of giving him a social life. With all his family commitments and his artwork, he really wasn't sure he had the time for one. Daz wasn't even Nick's friend – he was a member of Katie's band.

'Good. Now, sod off and find yourself a present before the shops close,' she commanded. 'I'll see you tomorrow.'

'Yeah. See you.' Nick put the phone away with a heavy heart. The shops would be closing in . . . He checked his watch and swore. Fourteen minutes. He left the Westfield Centre by the side doors and hurried out onto the street again, his shoulders hunched against the cold.

The streetlights had come on and the air taken on a new bite as late afternoon segued into evening. His stomach growled as the scent of somebody's takeaway floated past.

And he still didn't have a gift.

A goods van stopped to manoeuvre in front of him,

blocking his path. Rather than stand and wait for it, Nick turned left down a narrow side street. It was just the backs of shops along here, but it ought to take him down towards the market. Maybe he could get Julie a new purse or something.

He passed the kitchen door of a restaurant, grimacing at the rancid cabbage smell from the bins. Some unidentifiable liquid had been spilled there, so he crossed to the other side rather than walk through it.

The alley went on for a very long way. He must have overshot the market by now, but it was too dim to see for any distance ahead. If Nick didn't find a turn-off soon, he'd end up right over the other side of town. There was no way he'd get back to the market before the shops closed.

Should he go back? Nick hesitated and turned to see how far he'd come already. It was only because he stopped in that exact spot that he saw the sign at all.

Tucked away in the corner of an upper-floor window, the notice was almost buried in shadows and grime. It was hand-drawn in faded colours that must have once been bold, the fancy calligraphy making

him think of fairground rides and old-fashioned
advertising boards. The message was just one word –
Bargains.

It could have been the name of a shop or perhaps
simply a promotion. It could have been left there
decades ago by a business long since vanished. But
right now Nick was desperate enough to try anything.

The only entrance he could see looked like an
ordinary front door, though it had no number or letter
box. It was painted black, or maybe dark green; it was
hard to tell in the dim light, and much of the colour
had flaked away. There was a large cast-iron knocker,
but Nick was reluctant to use it. What if this was
somebody's home?

He gave the door a tentative push with his fingertips, half hoping to find it locked so he could turn and
leave. Instead it swung open with a sound that was
more a whisper than a creak. Inside was a featureless
hallway. Though the naked light bulb swinging from
the ceiling was lit, the walls were only exposed brick
and the floor concrete.

Nick hesitated on the threshold, more unsure than
ever. This was probably a delivery entrance. There

was no sign saying PRIVATE or EMPLOYEES ONLY, but it didn't quite look open to the public either. Was he allowed round here?

On any other day he would have let the door swing shut and moved on. Today he picked his way along the corridor, all too conscious of the echo of his footsteps. He shouldn't be here. Any moment now, some big bloke in a uniform was going to pop up and demand to know what he was doing.

Nick rounded the corner and found another length of corridor. Up ahead on the left was a low doorway. As he approached, he saw that the word BARGAINS was carved into the stone lintel above it. The stark, angular form of the letters made him think of Roman numerals.

He still wasn't sure this was a public entrance, but he walked on through it.

It meant taking a step down, and Nick had to twist his body awkwardly to get through the gap without cracking his head. The room he entered had the musty smell of a second-hand bookshop.

It had the look of one too: tall wooden shelf units lined all four walls and divided the room into dimly lit alcoves – but they weren't filled with books. Nick had no idea how the units could have come in through that door, since they were all solid hand-crafted wood, not the kind of thing that came in a flat-pack. The shelves all held the same thing: rows of polished glass orbs, racked up one behind the other like bowling balls.

They were all the same size, just a fraction too big to hold comfortably in one hand, and they were a translucent white, like frosted glass. There were no signs or labels anywhere to explain what they were, or if they were even for sale.

Curious, Nick picked up the nearest orb. It felt oddly warm in his palm, as if the glass had been sitting out in the sunshine instead of down in this cold little room. It was heavy, and he quickly shifted to a two-handed grip, afraid that he would drop it.

He peered into the orb. It was like stepping through fog. An image emerged at the centre of the ball, unclear at first, but then steadily sharper. It was a tiny, but amazingly detailed, scene of a garden in full bloom. Little trees, coloured flowers, a pond with rushes and lilies . . . it almost seemed like he could pick out individual blades of grass. The colours were dazzling yet still true to life, like in some award-winning photograph. The picture was so vivid that it yanked summer from Nick's memory by the roots, filling his mind with the sticky-orange taste of ice lollies and the smell of freshly cut grass.

Nick stumbled a little as he put the globe back, half surprised to find himself indoors. He grabbed for the next orb with clumsy fingers, suddenly desperate to see what was in it.

This one held a picture of a violin – no less detailed than the summer garden scene. He'd never touched a violin in his life, but as he gazed into the orb, he could almost feel the weight of the instrument; the shape of the calluses it had left on his fingers, different from the ones he got from drawing. He could sense the expectation of the unseen audience settling over him like a thick blanket. And there was . . . not just music, but the knowledge of how to *make* music, waiting in his head and hands to be released.

Replacing the orb on the shelf was a strangely melancholy thing, like packing away his old baby toys.

Nick wandered around the room, lifting orbs from

their holders at random. No two images were the same, even when he took the globes from the same rack. He found a beautiful snowy landscape, a woman holding a baby, a galloping horse – even a coffin. And every picture, no matter how distant from the life he led, seemed to come with strong sense memories and powerful emotions attached. By the time he'd looked at half a dozen he felt drained and not all there, like he'd just staggered out of the cinema after hours immersed in a film.

He tried to blink away the bleariness, and reminded himself of why he'd come. Julie. He was looking for a present for Julie. One of these orbs would be perfect, provided they didn't cost the earth – or even if they did. They were so amazing Nick felt like he *had* to have one, if only to stop himself coming back to the shop every day to stare at them some more.

He thought of the garden picture he'd seen first, but he couldn't work out where he'd found it. Picking up what he thought was the right one, he found himself looking at a storm-tossed sky. A jagged bolt of lightning forked down from blue-black clouds; he could smell the rain and hear the thunder and taste the electricity. His skin itched feverishly, and all the fine hairs on his arms stood on end.

'Have you made your choice?'

The voice came from right beside his ear, and Nick jumped and spun round, his heart pounding. There was a doorway in the alcove behind him that he hadn't seen before, and the man who'd spoken had come up so close that Nick had to hop away to be at a comfortable distance from him. He was shorter than Nick – and no one would ever have called Nick tall. Even so, there was something very intimidating about him. His stern, craggy face could as easily have been a weather-beaten thirty-five as a young sixty, and his eyes were such a dark shade of brown it was hard to tell iris from pupil. He wore a double-breasted suit that was surely hand-tailored, and his steely-grey hair was cropped like an army officer's.

As Nick stared at him, the man stared right back, scrutinizing him so closely that he straightened up automatically. He felt like he was being given a uniform inspection without having been told all the rules. He half wished he'd thought to put on a fresh shirt instead of the one he'd worn yesterday.

Just as the silence had grown so thick that Nick wasn't sure how to break it, the man spoke.

'You have an artist's hands,' he observed. It didn't sound like a whimsical comment; it was more like a TV detective barking out the clue that nailed the murderer. 'Do you draw?'

'Er . . . yes, sir,' he said blankly.

'Let me see.' The shopkeeper held out a hand towards Nick's bag as if certain that he would have examples in there. To his own bemusement, Nick found himself opening up the side pocket and handing over his sketchbook.

He shifted uncomfortably as the man browsed through it. What the hell was going on? He'd come here to buy, not be given an interview. Had he accidentally stumbled into some obscure little art gallery?

His skin burned with embarrassment at the thought. He knew he was good, but he'd rather have run all his sketches through a shredder than put them up to be judged against the standard of the orbs. Compared to this kind of art they might as well be finger-paint and scribbles.

14

'Hmm.' The man paused for a long time over the best sketch in the book, a view of the university campus from Brett's Hill. 'You have a certain amount of talent,' he allowed finally. He angled the sketchbook at Nick. 'Would you be willing to trade it?'

'What?' Still caught in wild thoughts of top-secret galleries, Nick wasn't sure he understood the question.

The man waved the campus sketch at him impatiently. 'This, for that.' He jerked his head at the orb Nick was holding. 'Will you accept the deal?'

'Oh! I, um . . . OK!' The university sketch was one of his favourites, but he wasn't crazy enough to turn down a deal like that. No way was his whole sketchbook worth a fraction of one of these orbs. Either the shopkeeper was gambling on the long shot of a Nick Spencer sketch being worth money one day, or he was simply out of his mind. He had to be some kind of eccentric, keeping these fantastic pieces of art tucked away in a back-alley shop that couldn't have seen much trade.

'Then we have a bargain.' The man extended a hand for him to shake. Nick awkwardly juggled the orb to his other hand in order to take it.

The grip was firm and professional rather than a hand-crusher, but he sensed there was a latent strength behind it. As the man pulled his arm away, Nick glimpsed a dark metal bracelet under his sleeve. It didn't seem to go with the smart suit – but then, a whole lot of things about this shop were pretty odd.

As the man carefully tore the page loose from the sketchbook, Nick was gripped by a sudden, irrational urge to snatch it back. It wasn't too late to change his mind, to refuse to accept the deal . . .

But why would he do that? It really was a bargain. If he couldn't bear to let go of one of his sketches for this clear a profit, how could he ever hope to make it as a professional artist?

So he gritted his teeth and let the man finish tearing it out. When he was done, the shopkeeper held the sketch up to examine it, handing the book back to Nick without even glancing his way. Apparently their conversation was over.

Nick stood awkwardly for a few moments, and then said, 'Right, um . . . thank you,' and slunk away.

He traipsed down the cold outer corridor. The

alley outside was now black as midnight, and the town had gone quiet and still. He was going to be very late home.

But at least he'd found Julie a present.

Nick let himself into his dad's house, the casserole smell emanating from the kitchen making his stomach grumble hopefully. Heavy guitar music from upstairs fought with the subdued murmur of the TV from the living room.

His father stuck his head out of the kitchen doorway. 'Oh, you're here,' he said. 'I thought you'd gone to your mum's and forgotten to tell me.'

'No, um' – Nick glanced over his shoulder towards the living room and lowered his voice – 'I had to get a present for Julie.'

'Oh, right,' his dad said in similarly conspiratorial

tones, then louder, 'dinner'll be about five minutes. Can you tell Kyle?'

'OK.' Nick trotted up the stairs. He thumped twice on his half-brother's door, but couldn't tell if his voice had made it through the volume of the music, so he twisted the handle and pushed it open. Kyle was slouched on the bed reading a comic, his hair flopping over his eyes.

'Dinner, five minutes,' Nick mouthed, adding makeshift sign language as backup. There was no point trying to talk over whatever metal band was screeching out of the computer speakers. Kyle gave him an absent-minded thumbs-up and dropped his eyes back to the comic.

Nick moved on to his own room. As he slipped off his coat, he went to the desk to check he really had written the date of Daz's party down. He used his school homework planner as a general life planner, because otherwise he was forever running back and forth between his two houses picking up books and clothes and bits of art equipment. He was still flicking through his scribbled notes for the next week when his dad yelled that the meal was ready.

It was only afterwards, while Dad and Julie were still downstairs doing the washing up, that Nick thought of the orb again. He closed the bedroom door and took it out to study.

Under the light in his bedroom, the glass appeared to be solid and milky white, and it seemed to take longer for the image to emerge – or else he was just impatient to see it again. The stormy sky was as compelling as it had been in the shop, but he couldn't help but feel that there was something subtly different about it. Had the lightning bolt always been striking a tree? He could swear that when he'd looked into it before there had been just the clouds and the lightning.

Nick shook his head. How could it possibly have changed? Maybe it was some kind of hologram that looked different from different angles. He rotated the ball a couple of times, and was perplexed to find that no matter which way he held it, the picture inside was always the right way up. How did it work? Some trick with mirrors or a weighted inner ball? He'd never seen anything quite like it.

Why were these orbs hidden away in a shop no one

knew about, with a shopkeeper who would give them away for next to nothing? They could be selling for millions! Nick only *wished* he could draw pictures that were half as evocative.

He remembered the first one he'd picked up – how it had yanked him from a crisp February evening into the midst of a perfect summer from his childhood. If he closed his eyes, he could still feel the sun warming his face and smell the blossoming flowers. He reached for his sketchbook, wondering if he could capture any of these feelings on paper.

Twenty minutes later, the page was still as blank as when he'd started. Nick set the pad aside with a groan and stretched his neck. Apparently he wasn't getting any drawing done tonight. Resigned, he tucked the orb away in his sock drawer and went to see what Kyle was doing.

Monday was, oddly enough, Nick's favourite day of the school week. He had to doze through English and history first thing, but after that he had double art and then PE in the afternoon.

When the eleven-o'clock bell finally rang, he

stopped pretending to care about factory reform and pushed his way out through the crowds, looking for Katie. Her orange puffy coat and dramatic gestures were easy to spot, even all the way across the playground. He made his way over to the bench where she was demonstrating a guitar solo with her school bag and a bottle of Coke.

'Nicky!' she called out as she spotted him, sitting up and kicking the bag to the ground. 'Did you manage to get a present?'

'Yeah, I did,' he said as he approached the bench. 'Coming to art?'

She checked her watch as she smoothed back her dark hair. 'Yeah, might as well. See you later, Lauren. Jodie – I'll talk to you at lunch, OK?' She threaded her way out from a big mob of girlfriends and slung her bag over her shoulder as she fell into step beside him. 'So *did* you buy her a cactus?' she asked.

Nick smirked. 'No, sorry. In the end I just got her a' – he waved his hands vaguely – 'pretty . . . gifty . . . thing from this little shop down by the market.' He didn't know how to put the orb into words in a way that would capture the wonder of it.

Katie snorted at him and teasingly copied the hand-waving. 'Oh, right. A *pretty gifty thing*. Come on, Shakespeare.' She shoved open the door to the art block.

They reached the top of the staircase just as the bell went, and Nick was first into the classroom.

Mr Henderson greeted him warmly. 'Morning, Nick! It's yet another still life, I'm afraid,' he said, gesturing to the arrangement of objects in the middle of the room. 'I know you can do this sort of thing in your sleep, but we do need to build up those course-work portfolios.'

Katie groaned as she walked in and saw the setup. 'Oh, God, not more *bottles*. I have two hundred and fifty-seven drawings of bottles! Sir, can't we draw something else?'

Nick didn't really mind all that much. It was dull, but at least it was practice, and any kind of drawing beat maths or essay-writing hands down. He sharpened a couple of pencils as the rest of the class came in, and then got down to work.

Only . . . he couldn't.

He stared at the random collection of objects,

waiting for something to happen. Katie was right, it was bog-standard stuff: old bottles and tins, a vase full of brushes, some artfully draped stripy cloth . . . It was nothing that they hadn't done a dozen times before. In fact, he'd had to draw that curvy blue bottle in at least two other art lessons.

And yet today his brain wasn't getting it. He could see there were shapes and shadows and textures, but they were all just hitting his eye in random splashes – there was no sense of cohesion, no overall pattern. It was like the opposite of finding pictures in the clouds; he was looking at something real and concrete, but seeing only meaningless chaos.

Nick blinked and tried to refocus. He stole a sideways glance at Katie's paper. She'd already blocked in most of the major shapes and started filling in the detail on the vase. He forced himself to concentrate.

OK, so he wasn't in the mood to draw. Sometimes he just wasn't – though this was more severe than usual. All he could do was force himself to pick out a part of the image and *get started*. He stared at the bottle to the left and made a few determined pencil strokes.

Then he had to stop and rub them out, because they were far too dark and at entirely the wrong angle. What was wrong with him today? This was so basic he ought to be doing it on autopilot.

Nick redrew the line, but it quickly went askew. He rubbed it out a second time and took a good long look at the bottle to fix the angle in his mind before trying again.

'Bloody *hell*,' he moaned in disbelief as the lines went wrong yet again. He gave up on the bottle, and focused on the tin at the front instead. Outlining a nice, simple cylinder shape – how could that go wrong?

Well, apparently by being lumpy, out of perspective and too high up on the paper. Nick tore the page off the top of the pad and balled it up. He yanked far too hard and it ripped instead of pulling cleanly out of the binding. He snatched irritably at the little scraps of paper remaining.

'Everything all right, Nick?' Mr Henderson raised a curious eyebrow as he passed by.

'Yes, sir,' Nick lied as he got up to toss the wad of paper in the bin. 'Just . . . didn't like the way it was turning out.'

'All right.' The teacher left it at that, sure that Nick Spencer wouldn't be messing around in an art lesson.

And he wasn't. He just *couldn't do the work.*

The second page remained as tauntingly blank as the first. Nick couldn't even bring himself to put a pencil to it. It wouldn't work, he could already tell. He couldn't do it.

To his humiliation, he could feel frustrated tears beginning to form at the corners of his eyes. He tightened his face into a glare to force them away. He pressed his thumb into his putty rubber and moodily studied the imprint that it made. Katie glanced up at him.

'What's up?'

'Nothing.' *Her* drawing, he could see, was already half complete. They'd been in the class for about fifty minutes, and he still hadn't drawn a single line. He'd never been so miserable to be faced with the second half of a double art lesson.

Nick sighed and reached for his pencil again. He *had* to do this. Even if he thought it looked awful, he just had to force it out somehow.

But he couldn't.

He doodled random patterns instead, rubbing them out when they started to overlap. Even those looked ugly and badly spaced. He couldn't produce anything but total crap.

With half an hour still to go before the end of the lesson, Mr Henderson came round again. 'Nick? You don't seem to be drawing . . . ?'

'I'm sorry, sir.' Those *stupid* tears were threatening to come back, and he hated the way they clogged up his voice. 'I think I'm getting a migraine.' As he spoke, he realized it might even be true. The whiteness of the paper seemed glaringly bright, and his gritted teeth were making his head throb. The smell of pencil shavings and the hubbub of the classroom were making him nauseous and dizzy.

'All right.' The art teacher's voice was soft and sympathetic. 'Do you want to go and sit in the sick-bay?' Nick just nodded, not trusting his voice any more. 'Pack up your stuff then.'

He collected his things in a hurry, painfully aware of all the speculative eyes on him. Katie offered him a concerned smile, but he avoided meeting her gaze. The more furiously he told himself not to get upset in the middle of the classroom, the more his eyes started to sting. He had to get out of there.

Nick fled into the corridor and down the stairs, his feet thundering on the steps. He came to a halt outside the double doors at the bottom, trying to get his ragged breathing under control.

This was crazy. He'd lost his ability to *draw*. What the hell was wrong with him?

III

Nick spent the rest of the lesson sitting in the sickbay, but he let himself be turfed out come the lunch bell. He would much rather have gone home, but the school would call his dad to collect him, and he was probably in the middle of getting things ready for Julie's party. It wasn't fair to mess up her birthday when he wasn't really ill.

He avoided Katie all through lunch by lurking in the library. They had basketball together in PE that afternoon, but Nick hung around in the changing rooms for long enough that the game was in progress by the time he came out. He just didn't feel like talking.

Unfortunately, thinking was a lot harder to avoid. Nick couldn't stop obsessing over what had happened in art. Why hadn't he been able to draw? Was it some kind of mental block? What if it didn't go away? Art was the only thing he'd ever been really good at.

He knew it was stupid to get so worked up after a single bad session, but he couldn't stop himself. What if he was still blocked by the time his art GCSE came around? It was only two months away – and they were supposed to be starting preparatory studies for it next week! Would they still let him into college if he ballsed up the exam? And what good would that do him, if he couldn't draw so much as a stick figure when he got there? He'd be kicked off the course before Christmas.

Nick ran himself ragged on the basketball court, trying to escape the feeling that his future was crumbling around him. By the time school was over he was so exhausted he barely managed to get changed and limp back to his dad's house.

As Nick entered the kitchen, he found every available surface filled with foil-covered plates of food. His father had been cooking and was just wrestling a tray of something spicy-smelling from the top oven.

'Ah, Nick!' he said jovially. 'Good timing. Can you put together a salad? I've got to see how long I need to cook these potato wedge things for.'

'Sure.' Nick would rather have gone up to his bedroom and sulked, but he dutifully dumped his bag and coat out in the hall and went over to the chopping board. He picked up a knife and took his frustration out on a cucumber.

'Don't let Kyle steal any more food. At this rate there's going to be nothing left by the time Julie gets here. Yeouch! Ow. Ow.' His dad scorched his fingers shifting meat patties from the baking tray to a plate, but continued to move the rest anyway. 'So how was school?'

'It was OK.' *Chop. Chop. Chop.*

His father was too frazzled to notice Nick's mood. 'How's the coursework situation going? Any more due this month?'

'No. I'm more or less caught up now.' The next thing on the agenda was the prep work for the art exam. He'd hardly even thought about it because he knew it wasn't going to give him any trouble.

The cucumber pieces had got ridiculously small. Nick swept them into the salad bowl with his knife and started attacking some celery.

'Good, good. I'm glad you're still keeping on top of things.' His father stepped back and rubbed a hand through his speckled grey beard. 'Right. Now, tell me. What have I forgotten to cook?'

Julie wasn't much of a party person, so her birthday do was really just a gathering of Nick's two families. Oddly enough, his mother and stepmother had hit it off quite early on, and now they were, to all appearances, fast friends. What James thought of hanging out with his wife's ex-husband, Nick was less sure, but his stepdad was laid-back enough that there was never any noticeable tension. Maybe it was a weird arrangement, but it was the one Nick had grown up with.

'Miranda, hi! You look lovely.' Julie greeted Nick's mum at the door. 'And James – oh, is that for me? Thank you.' She accepted the bottle of wine from him and gave him a kiss on the cheek. Nick's half-siblings, Greg and Rachel, scrambled past into the hall.

'Where's your party hat, birthday girl?' Nick's

mother shook the rain from her hair as she bounded inside. 'Sorry, I'm dripping all over your carpet. It's chucking it down out there – I swear, the sky was clear before we got in the car. Somebody up there must have it in for me. Oh, come on, Greg, move your bum. You're in the way.'

She and Julie seemed a mismatched pair. Nick's mother was a tiny little redhead with a fondness for loud clothes and flashy jewellery, while Julie was a tall bony woman who wore her blonde hair short and preferred to potter about the place in faded denims. Nonetheless, get the two of them together over a bottle of wine and they would soon be cackling like naughty schoolgirls.

'Can we eat now?' Kyle piped up hopefully from the table. Nick knew full well his half-brother had been stealing handfuls of food every time their father's back was turned. Their dad had pretty firm ideas about what he considered sensible eating, so it was rare to see so much junk food brought together in one location. Nick only wished he had the appetite to appreciate it himself.

'Presents first,' Rachel corrected him primly. She

was nine years old, and quite convinced that made her very grown-up. 'You have to open mine first, Julie!' She presented a shiny silver package that, judging by the mangled corners and ridiculous amount of Sellotape, she'd been allowed to wrap herself.

Which still put her one up on Nick. He grimaced internally as he realized that he was probably going to have to present the orb in a carrier bag. There was no way he had time to wrap it now, even if he'd had the paper.

He stood up. 'Er, mine's still upstairs.' He ran up to fetch it from his room.

As he lifted the orb out of his sock drawer, Nick took a moment to steal another look at the image inside. When it appeared, he frowned deeply. This time he was even more sure that the picture had changed. There was a fence. Since when had there been a fence? In fact, there was not just a fence, but a whole new line of trees and a leaf-strewn lawn beneath them too. And the closer Nick looked, the more he found himself thinking that it really looked *remarkably* like the trees outside his—

'Nick?'

He scrambled to his feet. 'Yeah, sorry! I'll be right down!' He grabbed a paper bag from the art shop out of the bin, smoothed it as well as he could, and put the orb in that. It was the best he could manage for packaging.

Nick returned to find the boys already making inroads on the food, and Julie dutifully exclaiming over a cuddly lion. 'He's so cute! Thank you, Rachel.'

'Get lost up there, did you?' Nick's mother teased, saluting him with her wineglass. He wrinkled his nose at the sharp tang of the alcohol.

'Couldn't remember where I put it,' he lied, embarrassed. He awkwardly handed the paper bag to Julie. 'Um, sorry it's not wrapped.'

'That's all right,' she assured him as she drew the orb out of it. 'You didn't have to— Oh, what's this?'

'You have to, er, look right into . . .' He moved to demonstrate, but she'd already raised it to face level to peer closer. A moment later, a smile of amazement broke across her features.

'Wow, that's beautiful. And it's so *tiny* – it's like a ship in a bottle. All that detail! Is it a picture, or an actual sculpture, or . . .? Will, you should have a look at this. Everybody, come and see what Nick's got me.' The other adults crowded round to admire the orb.

'It's got to be weighted somehow,' James decided, turning the glass ball over and over. 'Look, Miranda, the little trees stay the right way up whichever way you tilt it.' He shook it curiously, and Nick's mum took it off him.

'Didn't your parents ever teach you not to shake other people's presents?' she chided wryly, handing it back to Julie.

'That only applies while they're still wrapped up,' he defended himself, smirking.

'Oh, Nick, this must have cost you a fortune,' Julie said, almost reproachfully. 'You really didn't have to.'

Nick squirmed. 'Er, well, actually, the bloke gave me a discount because he took one of my sketches. So it didn't cost me that much.' He felt guilty taking credit for generosity he hadn't really shown, but he didn't want to sound cheap by admitting he'd got it for free, either.

'Really? He took one of your sketches? That's great!' His father beamed at him, delighted. 'See?

You're not even out of school yet, and you've got people interested in your art. Give it a couple of years and you'll be a gazillionaire.' He clapped Nick on the shoulder.

'He'll be keeping us all in yachts and mansions in our old age,' his mum said. 'I knew there was a reason I had children.' The others all chuckled.

Much to Nick's dismay, the conversation then turned to his artwork, and how well he was surely going to do in his GCSE. What would have been embarrassing on any normal day was excruciating after the art-class disaster, and he slipped away as soon as he could to join the kids at the table.

The party food made Greg and Kyle even more hyped up than usual – if that was possible. Nick's two half-brothers were both twelve and had long enjoyed confusing people by claiming to be twins – despite the fact that they had different surnames, different parents, and didn't look anything alike. Greg was a cocky little duplicate of James, his white-blond hair and silver-framed glasses giving him an angelic look he most definitely didn't deserve. Kyle had the same messy brown hair and dark eyes as Nick and their father, though his lanky build was definitely from Julie's side. He had his mother's laid-back temperament too . . . most of the time.

The two of them were deliberately winding Rachel up, stealing food from her plate and grossing her out with glimpses of half-chewed mouthfuls. Her indignant shrieks were piercing right through Nick's head. Combined with the grown-ups' laughter and the hammering rain outside, it was just too much for him to take. He filled up a plate and made his escape to the kitchen.

It was cooler out there with the lights off and the storm raging outside the windows. He watched droplets of rain make trails down the glass, backlit by flashes of lightning. Thunder grumbled like the low throaty growl of a big dog, lingering on for what felt like minutes. It really was a hell of a storm.

Even so, Nick half wanted to be out in it. It would be nice to stand and tilt his head back, feel the cold rain wash over his hot skin. He had the kind of raw headache you got when your nose was stuffed up from a cold, or because you'd been crying.

Not that he'd actually *been* crying. Perversely, that

thought made his eyes prickle, and he scrubbed at them irritably with a sleeve. The frustration he'd felt in his art lesson was so fresh in his mind that just remembering made his chest tighten. He still didn't understand how he could have frozen up like that. Even if he was completely uninspired, he should at least have been able to produce *bad* art. Not just sat there and scribbled like he'd never even picked up a pencil before.

There was condensation on the inside of the glass, and he used it to draw an angry face. Even that looked all wrong and lopsided. He smudged it out again with his palm.

The door behind him opened, spilling light into the kitchen, and he guiltily yanked his hand back from the glass. Julie entered with a bag full of wrapping paper to put in the bin.

'Oh, that's where you've got to. Noise getting too much?' she said knowingly. Nick gave a tight smile.

She leaned forward to peer up at the clouds. 'So much for "scattered showers",' she observed wryly. 'I think your mum's going to have to build an ark to get home if this goes on much longer.'

'Uh-huh.' He blinked in the wake of a particularly brilliant flash. The roar of thunder seemed to come only a heartbeat later.

He turned to look at Julie and saw that she was still carrying the orb. 'I was just showing your present to the kids,' she told him. 'It's lovely, Nick, thank you. Where did you get it from? I don't think I've seen anything quite like it.'

'Er . . . a gift shop in town. There was a whole range of them.' He was strangely reluctant to describe the full experience of Bargains. The parts that lingered in his memory were like the traces of a bizarre dream, the kind of thing you didn't tell in case it revealed too much about the way your brain worked.

'Oh, right.' Julie held the globe up in two cupped hands to admire it. Nick felt a strange and sudden tension, as if his hair was standing on end. He opened his mouth to stay something, but, before he could, some sixth sense made him whip his head towards the window.

A pillar of bright white light shot down out of the sky and seemed to dance for a moment up and down the trees by the side fence. Then there was a crackling boom – like the sound of an explosion.

I t took a moment for Nick to realize that the world hadn't shattered around him. The boom stretched out and rumbled on, transmuting into more familiar thunder. The dog from two doors down started barking loudly enough to wake the dead.

'That was a close one!' his dad exclaimed from the living room.

Nick turned round. '*Close?* It was in the back garden!' he said, his heart pounding violently in his chest.

'Will, I think it hit a tree,' Julie called, sounding as shaken as Nick felt. The rest of the family piled into a kitchen far too small for all of them.

'That was a hell of a bang,' Nick's mum said. 'I thought for a minute it had hit the house.'

'Let me see!' Greg tried to shove his way through to the front.

'There's nothing *to* see. It's dark.' Nick tugged him back down as he leaned over the draining board for a better look. 'It was, er, one of those trees over there.' He pointed vaguely, and found his arm was still trembling.

'I think it was the maple,' Julie said.

'Did it explode?' Kyle asked eagerly, squeezing past Rachel. She was happy to step back, looking distinctly pale in the dim light of the kitchen.

'That was really *loud*,' she said, huddling close against her dad.

James gave her a comforting squeeze. 'Yes, well, it's not likely to hit the house, so don't worry, OK?' he told her.

'Stay off the computers and the phone, all the same.' Nick's dad wasn't quite so quick to be reassuring. 'No games until tomorrow, OK, boys?'

'Oh, no!' Kyle protested. '*Dad*, it's not going to hit us. Lightning never strikes the same place twice, right?' He tried a winning smile.

44

'All right, come on, everybody out.' Nick's mum started herding the kids out of the kitchen. 'Back into the living room. Come on, shuffle, shuffle. There's no room to breathe in here.'

Nick and Julie were the last to leave, pressed as they were in the corner. His stepmother caught his eye and smiled. 'Well, you certainly know how to pick your presents,' she said, holding up the orb with a chuckle. 'Anyone would think you had this planned!'

'Yeah.' He forced a smile.

It disappeared the moment that she'd gone.

The crazy coincidence of the storm and the lightning strike nagged at Nick all evening, even when he tried to put it out of his mind. As he lay awake that night, the most wild flights of paranoia seemed credible. The image in the orb *had* been a picture of their back garden. His freeze-up in the art lesson was a sign he'd lost his drawing skills for good. The lightning strike had happened *because* he'd bought the orb. He was going to lose his college place and wind up unemployed and homeless.

Stupid, insane, pointless thoughts, but they kept his

mind busy most of the night. It seemed that Nick had barely slept at all when he was suddenly jarred awake by the sunlight spilling in through the curtains.

He forced his sleep-gummed eyelids open and squinted at the alarm clock. Still nearly twenty minutes until it was due to go off. Great. Not enough time to go back to sleep and too long to keep on ignoring his nagging bladder.

As he staggered unwillingly out of bed, he saw Kyle's door standing open. When he reached the bathroom, he could hear loud rustling coming from outside the house, so he opened the window and leaned out. 'Oi! What're you doing?'

He couldn't see round the side of the house, but Kyle called back, 'You've got to come and see this tree!'

Nick closed the window and went down to the kitchen, where the back door was also hanging open, letting all the heat escape. He stepped into his dad's wellies before venturing outside, but the bitter cold still stole his breath away. The grass was dusty white with morning frost, and the air was as sharp as ground glass.

Something with more substance than grass crunched underfoot, and he kicked at a fragment of bark. A few paces further on, he encountered another. This part of the garden was scattered with it.

The maple tree was all the way down by the end fence.

As Nick approached, he could see that there was a great long furrow gouged down the length of the trunk, as if someone had taken the bark off with a chisel. One of the big lower branches had splintered, and the end of it was dangling down. Kyle was out there in his too-small pyjamas and a dressing-gown, stretching up the trunk to try and grab the end of it.

'It's going to fall on your head,' Nick warned.

'No, it's not.' Kyle made a confident leap and managed to get a grip on the loose branch. Nick winced as he shook it, but it came free fairly easily, chunks of splintered wood raining to the ground. Kyle brandished the branch triumphantly, then prodded Nick with the end of it. 'Ha!'

'Oi.' Nick stepped back out of Kyle's range and raised a warning hand.

'All right, all right, no climbing the tree.' Their dad

had come out in his dressing gown. He rubbed his beard and grimaced as he surveyed the damage. 'Well, it's going to muck things up if that dies,' he observed. 'Next door'll be able to see right into our garden.' He clapped his hands. 'Come on, boys, away from the tree. There might be more loose branches up there. Get back inside before you freeze to death.'

Nick traipsed back into the kitchen, grateful to be in the warm again. As he levered the stiff rubber boots off, he could hear sounds that told him Julie was in the bathroom. He dropped the boots back where he'd found them and went into the living room.

The orb was standing on the mantelpiece, next to the misshapen clay dog Kyle had made in junior school. Nick approached it with some trepidation. What if the image inside really *was* a view of their back garden?

It couldn't be. Because that would make the orb . . . what? A crystal ball, capable of seeing the future? A bad-luck charm that had called the lightning bolt down on them? Either option was completely crazy.

He seized the glass globe in both hands, eager to get another look and banish his irrational worries. It was nothing but a big coincidence. It was just a picture. It was . . .

. . . Empty. Nick stared and stared into the orb, twisting it this way and that, but he saw only milky-white fog. It was as if the image of the lightning bolt had faded out of existence.

Or been used up, a little voice whispered at the back of his mind. There was the creak of a floorboard behind him, and he whipped round, eyes wide.

'Sorry.' Julie smiled kindly at his surprise. 'Bathroom's free.'

'Thanks.' Nick replaced the orb with shaky hands, and tried to convince himself that his goosepimples were just from the cold.

By the time he left for school, Nick had figured out several possible explanations for the missing picture. It could just have been some trick of the light or a reflection that stopped him from seeing the image. Maybe it was actually a battery-powered projection, and now the power source had gone flat. It could even have been damaged when the lightning struck – Julie might have shaken it, or perhaps the flash had somehow obliterated the image. There were dozens of rational reasons why it might have vanished.

He just wished his jittery brain would accept one of them.

The unsettled feeling grew and took on a new target as he contemplated his Tuesday timetable. He had double graphics fourth and fifth lesson, which would normally be the high point of his day. After yesterday's art lesson though, the thought of trying to do any sort of drawing in class made his stomach turn over.

He'd hoped this bizarre artist's block would be gone when he woke up this morning, but he was out of luck. In science, second lesson, he ended up rubbing out the diagrams over and over because he couldn't copy them properly. *Copying!* It was one step up from tracing. How could he mess that up? It was like he'd lost the basic motor skills that determined how hard to press, how to make the pencil go in the right direction. His lines wobbled, his proportions were all wrong . . . it just didn't come out right.

And yet he could *write* as cleanly and neatly as he ever had. The problem wasn't with his hand. It was in his head.

Nick looked at the wrinkled, graphite-smudged page. He couldn't even hide the evidence properly: his pencil control was so crap the lines were too dark to rub out completely. He surreptitiously tore out the page under the table, then went back and deliberately mis-numbered the questions so he could pretend he'd skipped the diagrams by accident.

His frustration soured the day for him, and he slipped away from his friends at break. He went to German early, hanging around in the corridor until the teacher arrived to let him in.

He was able to get a table by himself for that lesson, but in graphics he had Katie in his group again. He *really* didn't want any company right now, but it was a small class and there was no way to get out of sitting with her without making it obvious.

It was too much to hope that she wouldn't notice his dark mood. He was hunched over his drawing board with his shoulders so tense it was starting to give him a backache.

'What's up with you?' Katie asked, half an hour in. 'You've got a face like your brother ate your hamster.'

It was a toss-up which Nick wanted to do less – talk

or keep on pretending to work. He'd been inking over all the pencilled text on his project, the only task he could do that wouldn't require drawing. He didn't even dare ink over the illustrations, for fear that he would ruin weeks of work.

He sighed and capped his pen. 'Nothing. I'm just bored,' he said, spinning it in a circle on the desktop.

'Yeah, well, aren't we all?' Katie leaned back on her stool to check the clock on the wall. 'God, we're still only halfway through. And we've got another hour of this after lunch.' Nick groaned, and she looked at him sideways. 'Seriously, though – you usually *like* graphics, freak that you are. What's bugging you?'

'I don't know.'

He doubted he could explain his artist's block to Katie. She never had much patience with him when he was agonizing over a drawing; she would always be all, 'Oh, shut up, it's still better than I can do.' Katie herself had boundless self-confidence, and tended to assume that anyone who didn't was just fishing for compliments. She wouldn't believe for a minute that he literally *could not* draw right now, and she'd laugh out loud at the suggestion he might have lost the skill for ever.

So Nick shook his head. 'I'm just . . . not in the mood.'

'Another headache?' Katie guessed. 'You should get your eyes tested. You might need glasses.'

'I don't need glasses.' His eyesight wasn't the problem either.

'Or maybe it's a brain tumour. That would explain why you're in such a pissy mood. You've got giant pulsating growths pressing on your brain. *Squeezing* everything into a smaller and smaller space.' She made illustrative hand gestures.

Nick gave her a look. 'You know, that's what I like about you. You always know just what to say to cheer me up.' Despite his sarcasm, he couldn't quite help the beginnings of a smile.

Katie flicked back her dark hair. 'Hey, what can I say? It's a talent.'

She turned back to her drawing board, but Nick froze. The words triggered off a sudden memory of someone else's voice – of standing in that room with the wall-to-wall glass orbs, with the odd little shopkeeper holding his sketchbook and saying, *You have a certain amount of talent. Would you be willing to trade it?*

All of a sudden, the deal sounded very different from the one he thought he'd agreed to.

Nick shook himself. He'd clearly gone insane. Two days without drawing, and already he was seeing conspiracies? To take the words literally was beyond absurd. You couldn't *sell* someone your talent.

You couldn't buy lightning in a glass ball, either.

He felt queasy. It was a stupid, *stupid*, stupid idea, and yet now it had set in, it wouldn't leave him alone. The fact was, he'd been able to draw perfectly well on Sunday morning. Then he'd given his sketch away to the shopkeeper, and ever since then, he hadn't done so much as a doodle.

It *had* to be psychological. The double meaning of the shopkeeper's words had sunk in on some un-conscious level, and been leaped on by his inner anxieties. He had his college interview coming up, his art GCSE in two months . . . for the first time, his work was going up in front of external assessors who would actually *judge* it, not just pat him on the back and say well done for trying. Maybe the paranoid fear that he simply wasn't good enough had been waiting in the wings for an excuse to jump out and paralyse him.

He had to get that sketch back. It was simple enough: he'd just go back to the shop, tell the guy he was sorry but he'd already promised the sketch to somebody else and he'd pay whatever the glass globe should have cost. Then this stupid artist's block would surely lift.

By the time the end-of-school bell rang, Nick had become so keyed up with nerves that he thought he was going to puke. What if the shopkeeper refused to go back on the deal? What if the orbs were worth more than he could afford to pay?

What if he got the sketch back, only to find he still couldn't draw afterwards?

As he made his way downhill to the crowded town centre, even more irrational fears jostled for space in his brain. He wouldn't be able to find the shop. It would have closed down. The sign would have gone. The door would be locked up. After all, wasn't that how all the stories went? You bought something odd in a strange little shop, but when you tried to go back, it wasn't there.

The shop *was* there, though it took time to find it. Nick had to walk back and forth two or three times before he finally spied the Bargains sign in one of the upper windows. It wasn't visible at all unless you looked from exactly the right angle.

Nick was so convinced he would find the door locked that he almost jumped when it opened at his touch. He hurried along the corridor, chased by the echo of his footsteps on the concrete.

He found the room of orbs exactly as he remembered it. Somehow, it had grown more creepy in the meantime. The racks of glass balls looked like disembodied eyes; he felt as if the fog in them might lift at any moment, leaving him exposed to the gaze of who knew what.

There was no sign of the shopkeeper.

'Hello?' Nick said uncertainly. His voice only reached the volume of a whisper, but it still seemed too loud for this dead, airless space. All of a sudden he felt horribly claustrophobic, conscious of the lack of windows and how far from the street outside the corridors had taken him. He could easily be in an entirely different building to the one that he'd first entered.

He was sweating hard and he wanted to turn and run, but he steeled himself to approach the second doorway. Was that another section of the shop, or did it lead into some private back room? There was no cash register in the orb room, but he wasn't sure that meant anything. This was clearly not an ordinary business.

He peered through and found another length of featureless corridor. At the end of it a flight of stone stairs led deeper down. Just before them there was a door that stood slightly ajar, but not enough for Nick to get a look at what might be inside.

'Hello?' he said again, as if it was a charm that would excuse him for intruding. It seemed far too still and quiet for there to be anyone else here. He knocked softly on the door with his knuckles, then nudged it open.

It didn't go far, smacking up against some item of furniture. The room he was looking into was small, about the size of the walk-in supply cupboards they had at school, but nonetheless it seemed to be some kind of office. There were no windows, and the walls were an austere charcoal grey, bare except for a rectangular black clock with no numbers. Its tick was irregular, scraping over his taut nerves. A big, solid carved desk took up half the room, fighting for space with three large wooden chests.

On top of the desk sat Nick's sketch – and another of the glass orbs.

Nick felt a chill slide down his spine. For some reason, his stomach suddenly felt very funny. Instead of picking up his sketch, he reached slowly for the glass orb. If he peered into this one, what exactly would he see . . . ?

He didn't get to find out. Just as he was about to raise it to eye-level, there was a pointed cough from behind him.

Nick started, and the orb slipped from his shaky hands. He lunged to recapture it before it hit the ground. By sheer luck he actually succeeded, then slowly straightened up and turned round.

'Be very glad you caught that,' the shopkeeper said. His features were not obviously angry, but neither were they particularly friendly. 'You don't want to know what would have happened if you'd let it smash.' He plucked the glass ball from Nick's hands and returned it to the desk.

Nick froze, fishing for words. 'Um, I'm sorry! I

didn't mean to walk into your office. I just, er, I—'

'Had second thoughts,' the man completed with an exasperated sigh. 'Of course you did. Well, that's your concern, not mine. All sales are final and *quite* non-negotiable.' He turned to go, as if considering that the end of the matter.

'But . . . I made a mistake!' Nick blurted. 'I shouldn't have, um . . . I really need that drawing back. I'll pay you whatever the orb was meant to cost.' He reached for his wallet.

The shopkeeper gave a dismissive snort. 'Put your money away, boy,' he said coldly. 'There's nothing here you could possibly buy with it.'

Nick's legs were trembling with nerves, but he stood his ground. He *had* to get that sketch back. He just had to. All attempts to look at things rationally had burned away; he knew that until he had the sketch back in his hand, he was never going to be able to draw again.

'Please,' he said desperately. 'Just tell me what it's going to cost me.'

The shopkeeper looked up at the ceiling in a silent sigh. 'You *have* nothing that would be of any value to me,' he said, the tone clearly implying he was doing Nick a great courtesy by being so patient with him. 'You have no comparable skills, and no possessions of equal value. The shop won't take body parts from under eighteens.'

'*What?*' Nick couldn't help but yell.

'No, I don't care.' The shopkeeper held up a hand, as if expecting him to argue. 'You might think you're mature, but how long did it take you to start regretting *this* deal? You're too young to make life or soul debts. And that means you have nothing I consider worth my interest. The transaction stands.'

Nick stared at him blankly. The man was quite clearly insane. Soul debts? Body parts? What the hell did he think they were negotiating for? He wasn't a shopkeeper, he was a lunatic with an art collection. How was Nick meant to persuade him to part with the sketch when he was this far removed from reality? He might ask for the moon or an elephant or the secret of invisibility.

'There must be *something* I can do to get it back,' he pleaded.

'Do?' The shopkeeper's dark eyes narrowed, and

he smiled in a cold, thin way that Nick didn't like at all. 'Well, now. What you can *do* is a different matter entirely.' He went to the desk and opened a drawer. 'If you're willing to take out a contract of service to the shop . . .' He pulled something out of the drawer, but held it in his left fist so Nick couldn't see what it was.

As the shopkeeper turned to him, Nick took a nervous step backwards. 'What, er . . . what kind of service?' he said shakily. Artist's block or not, if the man even *looked* like he was going to try anything dodgy, Nick was making a break for the exit.

Which, he was painfully aware, was a long way away – down all those corridors.

But the shopkeeper just gave him another thin smile. 'You're far from the first person to be reluctant to pay what they owe. You'd be surprised how many of my customers mysteriously don't return when their time to pay up comes round. It doesn't get them any-where, of course – but it is inconvenient to have to go chasing them down.' He pursed his lips. 'It would be . . . advantageous to have someone else to make the collections for me.'

Nick's relief and incredulity mixed together into a

laugh. '*A debt collector?*' Of all the things he'd been expecting from this strange little man and his crazy-weird shop, that one hadn't made the top two million. 'You want me to work for you as a *debt collector?*'

The man looked him up and down and raised an unimpressed eyebrow. 'I shouldn't imagine you'll be any good at it. Nonetheless, I'm honour-bound to offer a term of service if the customer requests it. Accept it or don't – it makes little difference to me.' He folded his arms. 'If you want your art back, this is your only way to earn it.'

Nick hesitated for a very long time.

On the one hand, it was quite obvious his would-be employer had more than a couple of screws loose. And *debt collecting?* It was hard to think of any line of work he was less suited to. The first time somebody refused to pay up he'd probably apologize for wasting their time and run away.

On the other hand . . . His eyes were drawn back to the sketch on the desk. If this was his only chance to win it back and break this artist's block . . .

Well, turning the job down flat wouldn't get him anywhere. And it wasn't as if the agreement would be legally binding. If his drawing skills came back on their own – as they probably *would*, as soon as he convinced his superstitious half that there was a way to recover them – he could walk away without a second thought. It wasn't like he was going to be listing this on his CV.

Nick took a deep breath and extended his hand. 'OK. I'll take the job.'

The shopkeeper accepted it for a single hard shake. As he pulled their joined arms down, he suddenly slapped his left hand on top of Nick's wrist. Nick yelped in surprise as something cold and snake-like slithered over his skin. He yanked his arm back fast and stared at it, panicked. It had felt like something alive, but now he saw that it was a metal bracelet like the one the shopkeeper wore. It was closed so tightly around his wrist that he could feel his pulse reverberating through it. He flexed his fingers gingerly to make sure they weren't losing circulation.

Heart still beating rapidly with shock, Nick looked up.

'That bracelet marks you as an employee of the shop,' the man said, matter-of-factly. 'You'll be able to take it off when your term of service is complete. From now until then, you answer to me, and me only. You will do what I tell you, when I tell you, and you will not ask stupid questions. You may call me Mr Grey or Sir.'

He went over to the first of the three wooden chests and knelt down by it. He must have pressed a hidden catch somewhere, for the lid suddenly popped open. He fished a glass ball out of the chest and tossed it across to Nick, who fumbled and almost dropped it. 'This is your first collection.'

'It is?' Nick said, puzzled. He turned the orb over in his hands and then lifted it up to peer inside.

It wasn't like the ones in the front room. Instead of being filled with fog, this globe was fully transparent. There were tiny golden words engraved in the centre of the sphere – if *engraved* was the right word for lettering that seemed to just float in midair. Nick squinted, and saw that they read: *Craig Mullen, D12, Roger Bambridge Hall.*

It seemed like a hell of an extravagant way to record customer details. He frowned as the address penetrated. 'Isn't that one of the halls on the university campus? I won't be able to get in,' he pointed out. 'They have card locks on all the buildings.' He couldn't just walk into the block and knock on door D12.

And why was he even taking this 'job' seriously? It was probably a wind-up or some delusional fantasy. This guy Mullen might not have even heard of Mr Grey. He might not even *exist*. How was Nick supposed to follow the instructions of a madman?

'You'll be let in,' Mr Grey said curtly, without bothering to explain where or how. 'The customers know what they owe; make sure they shake hands on the deal, or any amount of verbal agreement is worthless. Bring the orb back to my office when the collection has been made.'

'You want me to go *now*?' Nick said, dismayed. 'I can't! I've got to be home—'

'You'll know when it's time.' Mr Grey folded his arms. 'Now, go. I don't expect to see you again until the job is done.'

He would know? How was he meant to know? None of this made any sense. 'But—'

'Go,' Mr Grey repeated, in a voice that brooked no argument.

Nick left.

As the conversation had taken deeper and deeper twists into the bizarre, he hadn't had time for much reaction except confusion. Now, though, as he stomped back along the corridor, his frustration and indignation started to build.

What the hell *was* this? Why should he have to jump through weird hoops just to get his *own* sketch back? It was Nick's right to decide if he wanted to sell it. He'd offered to pay the man back for it, and that should have been that.

This whole stupid debt-collecting thing was just some kind of scam to get a dirty job done without paying for it. If Mr Grey treated all his customers like he had Nick, it was no surprise they hadn't come back to settle their debts. Nick wasn't sure if the man was genuinely wacko, or just having fun at his customers' expense by making irrational demands.

Why had he even showed the man his sketchbook in the first place? He should have just said, 'Huh? No, I'm not an artist,' or pretended not to have his sketches with him. This was what you got for being polite and obedient and trying to get on with people – blackmailed into doing some ridiculous job that you were in no way qualified for.

Nick took a deep, shaky breath as he pulled the outer door open and stepped into the alley. He was relying on his aggravation to power him along, because some part of him, underneath the anger, was still extremely wobbly. It was like the dizzy, weak-kneed rush that came after a car had nearly swiped you off your feet, once you'd had a chance to stop and realize just how close it had come to hitting you.

Mr Grey had been too coldly indifferent for some-one who was pulling a wind-up. There had been no sly self-awareness there, no hint that he realized the things he was saying or doing might seem odd at all. He believed they were totally logical and sane. And that made him, in Nick's book, the scary kind of crazy. How could you know how someone like that was going to react?

Nick would have to be insane himself to consider following through with his *assignment*. If he had any sense at all, he'd get rid of the orb and the stupid bracelet, and never come back here again.

But . . . Mr Grey still had his sketch. If Nick truly believed it was the only way to break his artist's block – and by now, he was sickeningly sure of it – then he had no option but to play along. While he was under observation, anyway.

Nick stopped at a bench across from the Westfield Centre to study the bracelet that had been slapped on him. There was no reason to keep wearing it now that he was out of sight of the shopkeeper. If he wore it at home, people would want to know where it had come from – and what could he possibly tell them? He didn't think his parents would be very impressed with the agreement that he'd entered into.

Nick hadn't got too good a glimpse of the bracelet the shopkeeper wore, but he was pretty sure that his was its twin. It was about twice the width of a chunky watch strap, made up of interwoven strands of some dark metal. They came together in the centre to form the image of an eye within a star. It looked very old, like something you'd see in a museum display of Celtic or Viking jewellery.

Maybe it really was that old. Considering his

steadfast refusal to return Nick's sketch, Mr Grey seemed to be remarkably willing to hand out far more valuable works of art. Nick was still boggling over the fact that he'd made one of the orbs just to note down a customer's name and address. There was a line between doing things stylishly and going completely over the top.

The bracelet might have looked striking, but it really wasn't Nick's style – plus, it was an uncomfortable reminder of the crazy situation he'd been backed into. He would be only too happy to stuff it in the bottom of his bag and forget the whole thing for a few days – or weeks.

He tugged at the metal band, but he couldn't get it to budge. It fitted closely against his skin, and though the interwoven strips looked fragile, they had no stretch or give in them at all. What the hell was it made of? Nothing as soft as the usual jewellery metals, that was for sure. It felt more like iron or steel. The band was as unyielding as any pair of handcuffs.

Nick turned his wrist over, looking for the clasp, but there didn't seem to be one. There were no joins, no hinges, no cracks that he could try and insert a fingernail into. The whole thing was seamless, as if it had been made in one piece.

Which, of course, was impossible. He'd felt it close around his wrist. It had to open *somehow*.

Nick pressed, pulled, twisted and prised at every part of the bracelet several times over before he was forced to admit . . .

He couldn't get it off.

Nick kept working at the bracelet all the way back from town. All he got for his efforts was a ripped fingernail and a honk from a van that nearly ran him over.

There was obviously some secret trick to opening the bracelet – a particular sequence of movements, perhaps, or something with magnets. Whatever it was, Nick didn't know it, and he had a sinking feeling that short of taking a blowtorch to the thing, he was stuck with the bracelet until Mr Grey consented to take it off.

Added insurance to make sure that he went through with the job?

Nick let himself into his mum's house. He often stayed there during the week since it cut ten minutes off his walk to school. The trade-off for that was having to share a bedroom with Greg. As he climbed the stairs, he was greeted by a thunder of simulated explosions. Greg was glued to the computer, rambling away into his headset without even glancing at Nick. 'Yeah, look, there he is! That's the bloke who killed Ishi last time. Get him – no, you go round the base of the tower, I haven't got any ammo left on my— Oh, *well done*, Simon. You just shot me! I'm nearly out of life.'

Nick was fairly sure he could have got changed – or done just about anything else he felt like – without any risk whatsoever of Greg turning round, but all the same he grabbed his clothes and moved into the bathroom. He put on a baggy blue-green shirt that he'd inherited from his dad on the theory he'd grow into it someday. That day hadn't arrived yet, and probably never would. The shoulders were still far too wide for him, and the cuffs hung down over his hands.

That was exactly why he'd chosen it, but it proved to be a double-edged sword. Not only were the sleeves long, they were loose, and they had a tendency to slide back to his elbows if he lifted his arms too high. But he couldn't change a second time without exciting suspicion, so he had to eat his dinner hunched low over his plate.

'Are you all right there, Nick?' James asked him. 'You're a bit quiet.'

'Oh, er, yeah. I'm OK.' Nick managed a nervous smile. His bent position was giving him indigestion as he shovelled mashed potato down his throat as fast as he could. He just wanted to get away from the table and hide out in his room.

'So how was school today?' his mum asked.

Any recollection of what he'd done at school had been sandblasted away by his trip to Bargains. 'Um . . . OK,' Nick said blankly.

'Wow, you're a real font of information.' She smirked at him as she reached for the gravy. 'When is it your GCSEs start? April? Getting nervous yet?'

'I've only got art in April.' He tried not to grimace too visibly. 'The rest of them start at the end of May.'

'Oh, well. Art's all right.' James chuckled. 'That's not an exam, it's ten hours of you showing off, Nick.'

'Yeah.' Nick smiled sickly and squished his potato to death with his fork.

'How can you have a ten-hour exam?' Rachel asked dubiously. 'Do they make you stay after school? What if you need to go to the toilet?'

'They have a teacher come in and *watch* you while you're going,' Greg told her, with relish.

'*Whatever*, Greg,' she said disdainfully.

'They do!' He gave a defensive shrug.

As James explained the concept of having an exam run over multiple days to a sceptical Rachel, Nick hastily stuffed down the rest of his dinner and stood up.

'You must have been hungry,' his mum said, eyebrows raised. Nick made a noncommittal noise as he swallowed the last mouthful and took his plate out to the kitchen.

'Yeah, but how do they know you're not cheating?' Rachel was saying as Nick scraped the debris of his meal into the bin. He turned to drop his plate in the sink.

Without warning, the bracelet around his wrist suddenly grew blazing hot. His hand jerked up reflexively, and his plate and cutlery fell into the bowl with a loud clatter.

'Mind you don't drop it!' his mum called out cheerfully from the dining room. Nick didn't answer. The ring of metal around his arm burned like a radiator, getting progressively harder to bear as it stayed pressed against his skin. Where the hell was the heat *coming* from?

Panting, Nick wrenched the cold tap on and shoved his hand beneath it. Steam boiled off the metal as the water struck it, and for a moment his skin was blessedly numb. He jumped and shook his sleeve down quickly at the sound of the door opening behind him.

'Are you sure you're feeling all right?' James asked, frowning slightly. 'You look pale.'

'I, er – I've just got cramp,' he said tightly. The prickling heat was already beginning to return. He had to get out of here, fast.

'It's all that graphics work you do on the computer,' James said. 'You should take a break for a while. You want to be careful you don't give yourself a repetitive strain injury right before the art exam.'

'Yeah.' Nick barely maintained his grimace of a smile long enough to flee the kitchen.

He had no clear plan in mind as he thundered upstairs to his bedroom. Attack the bracelet with his craft tools, maybe; try to wedge some kind of insulation under it . . . The half-formed thoughts fell away into confusion as he registered the bright light spilling out from his doorway. He nudged the door further open with a foot, and saw that the glow was coming from inside his school bag, pouring from every gap in the canvas.

It had to be the orb.

With a panicked glance over his shoulder, Nick ducked in and slammed the door behind him. He fumbled with the buckles on the bag left-handed, shaking his right as the bracelet grew hotter and hotter. 'Come *on*, just . . . Ah!'

He finally got the clasps undone, and was almost blinded by the brightness of the light that flooded out. He groped in his bag blindly until his fingers closed around smooth glass.

The glow winked out.

As did the heat from the bracelet. One second it

was there, the next it was gone, without any kind of cooling period. The metal that had been burning him was suddenly soothingly cold against the skin it had just scorched.

Nick flexed his fingers carefully, and blinked away brilliant after-images.

What the hell was going on?

It had to be some nasty little trick of Grey's. Done with a timer . . . sensors . . . remote control . . . His mental list of explanations stuttered out. However the devices had been set off, the purpose was clear. His attention was being drawn to the orb. He raised it to eye-level slowly, and found that the message inside had changed. The name and address were still there, but beneath them it now read: *Tuesday 26th February, 8 p.m.*

Today. Nick's eyes went to his watch automatically. It was already half past seven.

Apparently, this was what Mr Grey meant by 'You'll know when it's time.' Nick swallowed. If this was just the method of announcing the appointment, what would the shopkeeper do if he failed to keep it? He eyed the bracelet balefully.

He jumped at a faint knock on the bedroom door behind him, and hurriedly stuffed the orb back in his bag. His mother opened the door and leaned in. 'You need to get ready in about fifteen minutes,' she said.

'What?' Nick stared up at her in confusion.

'We're taking Rachel skating,' she reminded him.

'Oh. Is that today?' he asked, wide-eyed with panic.

She frowned and curled her hand around the door handle. 'Is that a problem?' she asked, raising one thin eyebrow.

He'd never been a talented liar. 'I, um, I only just remembered,' he babbled. 'I said I'd go over to, um, my friend Rob's house and work on this . . . er, group project we're supposed to be doing. It's due in this week, so we've got to, um . . . I just forgot,' he said, as miserably guilty as if it really was his fault.

'Can't you work on it at school?'

Nick wriggled like a worm on a hook. 'Er, no, it . . . He's got it on his computer. This is the only time we can all get together.'

His mother let out a faint huff of a sigh. 'OK. Well, don't worry about it. You go on and meet your friends.'

'I—'

'Don't worry,' she said again, holding up her hands. 'It's not important.'

That only made him feel worse. 'I'm sorry.' He twisted his lip in an apologetic grimace.

She rolled her eyes and gently swatted him. 'Oh, for God's sake. Stop with the sad-puppy eyes. It's a skating trip, not your one last chance to see your dying relatives. Go on, shoo. Get lost and do your own thing. We can have fun without you.' She flapped her hands at him.

'Sorry,' he said again as he went over to pick his shoes up.

'And don't keep saying sorry,' she told him.

'Sorry,' he repeated, unable to suppress a smile.

His mother narrowed her eyes. 'Don't be a smartarse,' she said, only a small quirk at the corner of her mouth betraying the playful nature of the admonishment.

'Sor—'

'All right!' She threw up her hands. 'I'm going.' She turned on her heel and marched across to her own bedroom. 'Rachel, come on, you need to start getting ready!' she shouted down the stairs.

Nick's grin soon faded as he laced up his trainers. He wished he *was* just heading out to catch up on some school work. What was waiting for him at the university? And how much trouble would he be in if he failed to make his appointment?

He met James and Rachel on his way down the stairs. 'Aren't you coming with us, Nick?' James asked, adjusting his glasses.

'No, um, I've got to go round my friend's house to do some homework. Sorry, Rachel.'

She shrugged abruptly. 'I don't care. Dad, can we get hot chocolate and cookies after?' She hopped up the rest of the stairs.

James gave Nick a wry smile. 'See you later, Nick. I don't know, Rachel,' he said, following her up. 'We'll have to see. Make sure you wear a jumper – it's going to get cold.' His voice receded as he hit the landing.

'Greg!' His mother's voice rose to eclipse the others. 'I don't hear you putting your shoes on!'

'I'm coming!' Greg bellowed back from the living room, although the volume of the TV didn't fade at all.

'Bye,' Nick said to no one in particular, and left the house.

The night air was cold, verging on freezing, and he walked through the streets at a fair clip, trying not to think too much about what he was doing. It was crazy to even think of keeping this 'appointment' . . . but he couldn't forget the way the bracelet had heated up around his arm. Had it been triggered by some kind of timer, or was Mr Grey controlling it remotely? Could he use it like a shock collar if Nick didn't do what he wanted?

This was way beyond a twisted practical joke. Mr Grey was clearly dead serious about wanting Nick to do this job.

What would happen if he *didn't* do it? Nick wasn't sure he wanted to know.

As he approached the university campus, he soon became part of a crowd. There were students everywhere: trudging home to halls, headed for a late session at the library or computer labs, tumbling in or out of the on-site bars. They were loud and busy and purposeful and confident, and he felt like a little kid among them even though he was just a few years younger. Nick was short, slight and spotty, and he knew he didn't look eighteen. Every time he passed a group who exchanged a whisper or burst into laughter, he was sure he was the target.

Where the hell was Roger Bambridge Hall? The campus was a mess of funny-shaped and oddly positioned buildings, impossible to walk through in any methodical way. Half the turnings seemed to lead to the back end of nowhere, and the others kept taking him back to places he'd already been. He kept on walking anyway, too nervous about looking out of place to ask for directions or stop at the big campus map.

Finally, through luck and a sequence of turns he'd never be able to repeat, he found himself outside Roger Bambridge Hall. It was a large building with at least eight floors, and there was a lobby with a security desk. Thankfully it was unmanned. The main doors weren't locked, and he let himself in, swallowing as his heart pounded fast in his chest. He hadn't realized how much this was going to feel like a break-in. If the security guard came back now and found him loitering, he could be in serious trouble.

There was a door to the right that led into the building. That was the one with the card lock. Nick started towards it, and glimpsed someone coming along the corridor. He turned away quickly, pretending to search for the right key in front of the postboxes.

Two girls emerged laughing, dressed up for a night out. They breezed through the main doors in a blast of strong perfume without even glancing his way.

Nick felt like he was going to be sick.

He jumped as his watch bleeped the hour. He should be there already, but he still didn't know how he was meant to get past the card lock. Mr Grey had said he'd be let in – by who? Where? Was he even in the right place?

Nick checked that no one else was coming, then approached the door. He raised a hand to try it, well aware that it would be futile.

As his fingertips touched the painted wood, he felt a buzzing sensation from the bracelet around his wrist. It reverberated up through his hand, giving him pins and needles. He flattened his palm against the door, and heard the electronic lock click.

The light on it had turned from red to green.

Nick stared at it for a long moment, then gave the door a tentative push. It eased open.

He passed through and crept along the corridor, flinching as he heard the door shut behind him. He wasn't sure what had just happened. Was there some concealed circuit in the bracelet that had interfered with the lock? Or had some unseen person buzzed him through at a precisely chosen moment?

Both options were equally disquieting. How did Mr Grey have the resources to do all this? Was he some kind of local crime boss or something? What kind of business had Nick unwittingly stumbled into here?

All of a sudden, the idea of failing at his task was even more nerve-racking.

He reached a pair of lifts and jabbed the button for D floor, jiggling nervously on the spot as he waited. When the lift arrived, it was occupied by a bearded guy in an IRON MAIDEN T-shirt. He gave Nick a friendly smile as he stepped out. 'Hey.'

'Hi.' Nick managed a sickly grin in return. As soon as the lift doors closed behind him, his knees sagged and he let out a shaky breath.

Somebody else got in at the next floor up, a pretty Asian girl with pink hair who was far more interested in her MP3 player than in him. He was relieved when she didn't follow him out onto D floor.

There was a second card lock to get into the residential corridors from the lift area. He placed his hand over it, and again there was a buzz from the bracelet, followed by the green light. He passed through, hurrying as he heard a burst of laughter from the kitchen on his left.

There it was, coming up on the right: room D12. It looked just the same as all the other doors he'd passed. Nick loitered outside for a few moments, but there was no sound from within. Was there even anybody home? It was probably cowardly, but a big part of him hoped there wasn't.

He pulled the orb out of his bag and studied it. The message inside hadn't changed. He checked the room number three times, just to be absolutely sure.

But he hadn't made any mistake. This was definitely the place.

Nick knew he ought to knock, but he still made no

move to raise his hand. What was he supposed to say? He rehearsed the words in his head.

Hi, Mr Mullen? My name is . . . Should he even give his name? What if his target reported him to campus security or something?

Hi, Mr Mullen. I work for Bargains gift shop in town, and I understand that you . . . I'm here to collect . . . Mr Grey tells me . . .

Before Nick could lose his composure completely, he knocked on the door.

It was opened by the biggest guy he'd ever seen.

VII

On a second, more considered glance, the man wasn't actually that tall. He still had half a head on Nick, but that didn't make him a giant. It was the sheer weight of muscle that made him look enormous.

The sweatshirt he wore would have been baggy on any normal person, but it clung to his huge frame. He practically filled the doorway, his arms and shoulders so bulked up he could hardly let them hang comfortably against his sides. The thick-set, expressionless face and straw-like hair added to a look that wasn't especially attractive, but *was* hellishly intimidating. Nick swallowed and took a step backwards.

The wide forehead crinkled into a frown as the silence hung on. 'Can I help you?' he said finally.

Nick's carefully rehearsed words had dried up. 'I, er, um . . . are you . . . Craig Mullen?' For a horribly blank moment he couldn't even think of the man's name.

'Yeah. Who wants to know?' Mullen casually rested one hand against the doorframe, and Nick couldn't help but watch the way his muscles bunched and moved.

'Oh, I, er – my name's Nick Spencer. I work for Bargains.' He remembered to raise his right hand and display the bracelet.

'Oh.' Mullen's slightly hostile look fell away into something more anxious. It changed all the lines of his face. Nick looked past the muscleman build for the first time and realized that he couldn't be much beyond twenty. 'Um, right. I guess . . . come in then,' he said uncertainly.

He moved back from the doorway and gestured for Nick to come inside.

The university room was large for a bedroom, but fairly cramped for a living space. There was a corner sink with a stash of beer cans lined up under it, and crumpled laundry drying on a rack over the radiator. There was little furniture – a narrow bed, a wardrobe and a desk with a built-in bookshelf – but the room still felt claustrophobic with two people in it, especially when one of them was as big as Mullen.

There was one of Mr Grey's orbs standing at one end of the bookshelf.

Mullen shuffled backwards until he was resting against the window ledge and stuck his hands in his pockets. 'So what happens now?' he said nervously.

He was asking Nick?

'Well, I, er . . . you know what you're supposed to pay, right?' Nick was taking a shot in the dark, but it seemed to mean something to Mullen. He nodded his head rapidly.

'Oh, OK, I have to give you a . . . Right, hold on.' He crouched down to drag a cardboard box out from under his bed. 'I put it . . . It's in here somewhere. Just hang on a second.'

Nick hovered awkwardly by the door as Mullen

rooted around for whatever he was looking for. His eyes were continually drawn back to the smoke-filled orb on the bookcase. What kind of trade had Mullen agreed to, and did he still consider it worth it? Had he been tricked into giving away more than he'd intended to like Nick had? Nick had a sudden burning urge to talk the guy out of it, even though that was exactly the opposite of his assigned job.

'Got it!' Mullen said abruptly, scrambling up. He held out a small silver trophy for Nick to see. Nick was sure it couldn't be worth much, especially with Mullen's name engraved on it, but it obviously meant something to him. He gave a kind of embarrassed-but-proud smile. 'That was my first competition. I didn't think I was going to get anywhere. You should see the muscles on some of those guys . . . but it was really cool, actually.' He hesitated over handing the trophy to Nick, and his expression turned rueful. 'But I don't really have time to keep up with all the training anyway now, so . . .' He shrugged and held it out.

Nick took the trophy, feeling like scum. 'Are you sure?' he felt bound to ask. 'I mean, if you've changed your mind, maybe I can . . .' He trailed off, knowing his chances of persuading Mr Grey to relent were less than pathetic.

'Look, I *have* to pass this course, man,' Mullen said, sounding defensive. 'My dad's not going to pay for me to repeat the year. He already wants me to give it up and go back to working for him. I can't do that again! I'd go nuts. If I don't get at least a pass, my life is over.'

Nick could definitely sympathize now. 'Mr Grey's going to fix your grades for you?' he said dubiously.

'Hell, no,' Mullen said indignantly. 'I know my stuff. I could practically teach this class! I just . . . I freeze up when I'm sitting there with the exam paper in front of me, you know? I had to retake my A-levels twice. My dad thinks I'm a moron. That's why I took up body building in the first place. It's supposed to be, like, *tone the body, calm the mind* and all that. But it doesn't work. I tried everything. And then my mate Tommy told me about this shop that's supposed to be able to trade you absolutely anything . . .'

'You think Mr Grey can *sell* you some self-confidence?' Wow. The shopkeeper was a bigger rip-off merchant than Nick had realized. Did he get some kind of twisted kick out of playing mind games with his customers?

'I know he can,' Mullen said. 'I mean, I didn't really think it would work, but I took this mock exam today . . .' He shook his head. 'Man, it was like I was somebody else. I know I aced it. And I didn't even feel like I was going to throw up or anything.' He bit his lip, and his eyes flicked to the trophy in Nick's hand. 'So I guess now I have to honour my end of the deal.' He took a deep, shuddering breath. 'Is that it? I mean, do I just have to give you that, or . . . ?'

'Oh!' Nick remembered Mr Grey's instructions. 'Yeah, er, we just, um, we just have to shake hands to make it official.' But he hesitated, still uncomfortable. He supposed that if Mullen *thought* he'd been sold the key to self-confidence, the psychological effect was nearly as good, but he still didn't like taking something that obviously had sentimental value. He held up the trophy. 'I mean, if you're sure you want to give this up . . . ?'

Mullen looked like he was having second thoughts, but he gave a brief shrug. 'Hey, when am I going to need body building in biochemical engineering?' he blustered with a too-wide smile, and extended his hand. 'Let's just shake on it, man.' The unspoken *before I change my mind* was clear in his expression.

Nick still wasn't happy, but there were only so many times he could attempt to sabotage his own job. He took Mullen's hand cautiously, braced for what could easily be a bone-crushing grip.

As their hands clasped together, pain shot through his forearm – but it wasn't coming from Mullen's grip. The bracelet suddenly clamped tight around his wrist, cutting off the circulation. Hot energy blazed out from it, sending tingling ripples up and down his arm. The trophy bit into his palm. Nick gasped, hot tears filled his eyes, and the whole room seemed to warp for a moment; things became dark and blurry, as if glimpsed through muddy water, and the outlines of objects wobbled and lost their certainty.

Then everything suddenly snapped back to normal, and Nick straightened up, shaking his hand. The hot pain had cut out as quickly as it arrived, but it left a pins-and-needles numbness in its wake.

The force from the bracelet must have transmitted itself to Mullen, for he'd dropped to his knees and doubled over. 'You OK?' Nick asked, offering him a guilty hand up. 'Sorry. I didn't realize that was going to—'

He swallowed the rest of his words – and very nearly his tongue – as Mullen raised his head. It was as if Nick was looking at a totally different person.

Or perhaps not quite. It was more like Mullen had been suddenly and inexplicably switched for his identical twin; one who had the same genes, but had spent the past few years living a completely different lifestyle. His skin was two shades paler and his hair seemed less sun-bleached, as if he hadn't spent as much time outdoors. His features were the same, but set into a substantially thinner face . . . and the rest of his body was now a completely different shape.

Before he'd been an intimidating mass of muscle; now he was scarcely more built-up than Nick. The sweatshirt looked huge on his reduced frame, its shoulders sagging down so the sleeves were far too long for him. As Nick gave him a hand up, Mullen staggered sideways as if he'd forgotten how to control his body.

Or as if it wasn't responding with the amount of power he was used to.

'Whoa.' Mullen clutched hold of the side of his desk. 'It's like being drunk – only my brain works.' He turned and stared at himself in the mirror over the sink with a kind of horrified fascination. 'Holy Christ! I look thirteen years old!' He raised the baggy jumper to stare at the muscle-free chest beneath. 'Oh my God. I didn't think it would . . .' His face crumpled as if he was on the verge of bursting into tears, and Nick looked away hastily.

His mind was spinning like a car with its wheels stuck in mud, endlessly revolving through a loop of *That did not just happen, that did not just happen, that did not just happen . . .*

Mullen cleared his throat twice, drawing Nick's attention back to him. 'It's not so bad, right?' he said shakily. 'I mean, I can build it all up again. When I get the time . . .'

'Yeah . . .' Nick said, his tongue thick and heavy as lead. 'I'm sorry, I have to go,' he said abruptly, and bolted.

He ran all the way down the fire stairs and out of

the building, unwilling to stand still long enough to wait for the lift. They took him out of a side door into an area of the campus he hadn't passed through on the way in, but he kept going anyway, sprinting along the darkened streets until the flash of street-lights made him dizzy and a stitch forced him to stop. He wound up all the way over the opposite side of town, gasping for breath past the sick feeling that constricted his throat.

His head throbbed. None of this was possible. It was like the twisted logic of a dream – but it couldn't be a dream. He could feel the wheezing in his chest, smell early blossom on the trees beside him, look up and see a full tapestry of stars and shreds of cloud. Dreams didn't have this kind of detail, and they fell apart as soon as your logical mind woke up.

He was prodding and poking desperately, but things were refusing to fall apart.

Mr Grey wasn't a lunatic. He wasn't a weird old man selling pretty spheres and playing mind games. He had power. He could take things from people and make things happen.

And Nick hadn't given him a sketch. He'd given him his *art*.

The bag on his shoulder clinked as he shifted position. With quaking hands he opened it and pulled out the orb he'd been given. It was no longer transparent, but filled with a familiar white mist. He peered into it, and caught a very brief glimpse of muscle-bound arms and a torso before wrenching his gaze away and stuffing the orb back into his bag.

Nick tilted his head back and breathed in the night air, the cold doing more to clear his head than the taste of petrol fumes from the busy streets. 'OK,' he said out loud, for the reassurance of it. 'OK.'

Mr Grey had . . . power. Mr Grey had Nick's artistic talent. The only way to get it back was to play his game. Well, Nick could do that. He'd done tonight's mission, hadn't he? It hadn't been fun, but he'd done it. And he could do however many more it took to have his skill returned to him.

It wasn't as if he had any other choice.

He turned and started walking towards Bargains.

VIII

The town was spooky at this time of night. It wasn't even that it was particularly late, but though the Westfield Centre was shut, and the only places still open were selling fast food or alcohol. The smell of greasy food from the burger places made Nick's nervous stomach turn over.

He made his way along the darkened alley back to Bargains. He might never have found it by sight, but the bracelet on his wrist gave a faint tug when he neared the door, as if it was pulled by a magnet.

He'd stopped coming up with scientific explanations. He just followed the pull and let himself inside.

Mr Grey was waiting for him in the orb room. 'Do you have it?' he said curtly, without so much as a nod of acknowledgement.

'I, er, yeah.' Nick fumbled to get the orb out and handed it over along with the trophy. He endured a long, nerve-racking silence as Mr Grey held them up one after the other, turning them this way and that as he examined them for who knew what.

'Fine,' he pronounced eventually. 'Your next assignment is on the desk in my office. Get it and go.'

'I . . .' Questions were jostling for space in Nick's brain. *What are these things? How do I get this bracelet off? How many of these collections am I going to have to make? When can I have my art back?* They all dried up in the face of the shopkeeper's hostile impatience. 'Yes, sir,' he said miserably, then trudged through to the office.

There was another orb waiting for him on the desk. Nick picked it up and peered at the name inside. *Tariq Khalil, 17 Goldbrook Avenue.* No date or time had appeared yet. He tucked it into his bag.

As his gaze fell on the bare desk, he couldn't help but wonder what Mr Grey had done with his sketch and the orb that accompanied it. His heart lurched at the thought that even now his artistic talent might be sitting on a shelf somewhere in the front room, ready for anyone to walk in and buy. What if somebody took away his skills before he'd earned enough credit to get them back?

He made himself take a deep breath. There was no reason to think Mr Grey had put the orb up for sale – unless you counted the fact that he seemed to get a kick out of yanking Nick's chain. Maybe the shop-keeper had set it aside for him somewhere, to wait until he'd paid back his debt in service to the shop.

His eyes were drawn to the three wooden chests that stood against the side wall. They were solid, sturdy things that looked like they were built for security, but none of them had a visible catch or key-hole. Instead, each had a subtle pattern laid into the wood where the lock would be. It was the same symbol – an eye, within a star, within a complex knot – that adorned the metal bracelet he was wearing. After a nervous glance back towards the orb room, Nick stepped forward and laid his palm over the pattern on the first of the chests.

The bracelet around his wrist vibrated softly, and

the lid suddenly bounced upward a little, as if someone had been pulling hard on the underside and had only just let go. Still watching the door, he eased the chest open.

It was almost a disappointment to find it filled with yet more orbs. Nick could see at a glance that the one that held his art skills wasn't among them. These orbs were all transparent, holding only names and addresses instead of the fog that filled the ones in the front room – debts that had yet to be collected. He winced at how many there were in the box. Would he have to collect all these himself?

He shut the chest carefully, and moved on to its neighbour. More of the same, although this one was less full. Some of the orbs didn't even have names in yet. They were just empty glass spheres. Nick wondered if Mr Grey did his own glass-blowing, or if some company somewhere was churning out glass bubbles without a clue what they were being used for.

Or maybe there was a whole industry supporting shops like this all over the world. He suppressed a shudder.

Mr Grey still hadn't come to see what was taking

him so long, so he risked moving on to the final chest. Maybe items held in reserve would be in this one.

Nick wasn't exactly sure what he would do if he *did* find the orb containing his art skills. Snatch it up and run? That would probably be fatally stupid . . . And there was no guarantee that just *having* the thing would allow him to access what was inside. Even so, he was strongly tempted. He had no idea what kind of crazy world he'd stumbled into here, but he would be only too happy to stumble out again – fast.

It was a moot point, anyway, because while the third chest held – yes – even more orbs, they were different from the ones he'd seen so far. These were made with thicker glass, and they came in a variety of sizes, from golf ball up to watermelon. The mist inside them came in different colours, and in some it was swirling quite dramatically.

Speciality items of some sort? The curiosity was overwhelming, and Nick had to raise a purple one up to eye-level to peep inside. What could count as extraordinary in a shop like this?

The indigo mists parted, and he was falling

forward – falling, falling, falling, as rapidly as a bungee jump, hurtling without brakes towards a huge, dark, devastated cityscape. He glimpsed the burned-out shells of skyscrapers, empty streets choked with rubble and ashes, and black clouds in a blood-red sky. And as his field of view rotated to show him the horizon, he saw —

A hand suddenly clamped over the glass. The orb was plucked away from him.

'I said *desk*,' Mr Grey said pointedly. 'Not chest. If you'd dropped that ball, the results would not have been pretty.' He returned it to the box with extreme care. 'Now go.'

Nick didn't stick around to push his luck.

It had started to rain while he was in Bargains, and before he was out of the town centre the scattering of droplets turned into a downpour. He felt dazed, as if he had a high fever. Everything around him seemed slippery and insubstantial. He felt like if he turned round fast enough, he would catch the edge of the illusion. Only the fact he was so cold and wet made him sure this wasn't a dream.

And he could feel the weight of the bracelet around his wrist: it was real. Mr Grey was real. Craig Mullen was real.

The bargain was real. Work for the shop . . . or never draw again.

Nick stopped and flexed his hand, watching the bones and muscles move under his skin. He saw now that the calluses on his fingers were faded, almost gone. He hadn't noticed before: when you knew something as well as your hand, you didn't even look at it. But they were gone, like Mullen's hard-earned muscles: the physical record of years of hard work erased in a heartbeat. Stolen from him.

Mullen had said he'd be able to build the muscles up again, but Nick wasn't so sure. He had a feeling that when Mr Grey bought something from you, it stayed bought.

What was it that he'd seen in the purple orb he'd picked up in Mr Grey's office?

Something he sincerely hoped no one could ever afford, or want, to trade for. Nick thought again of the lightning bolt crashing down on the maple tree. How easily could he have called it down on the house, on himself – on someone else? It would have been the perfect murder weapon.

What kind of people bought things from a shop that could sell anything? The desperate . . . and the dangerous. The sort of people who might not take too well to being informed that their own end of the bargain was due.

But what choice did he have except to take the deal he'd been offered? Nick let his sleeve slip back and studied the bracelet. It looked less like a piece of jewellery now than it did a manacle. It had powers beyond anything he understood – but *he* wasn't the one in control of it.

By the time Nick made it back to the house, much later than he'd intended, he was wet through. Greg was still up and tapping away at the computer keyboard, but Nick was so exhausted he crawled into bed anyway, with barely a mumbled greeting to his half-brother. He was asleep long before Greg turned out the lights.

He slept through the night without dreaming.

Morning seemed to come round far too quickly. Nick could barely keep his eyes open at breakfast. He stirred his cornflakes without any enthusiasm; he had a raging headache, and he was slowly cooking, sat in front of the heater with his school jumper on. He'd had to get fully dressed straightaway, because the T-shirt he slept in was short-sleeved. If he was still stuck wearing the bracelet when summer rolled round, he was going to have a major problem.

Make that two major problems, because the art exam was only a couple of months away. They were meant to be starting on the prep work for it next week. Could he possibly earn out his debt to Mr Grey before then?

'Did you get that work finished?' his mum asked, breaking into his thoughts.

'Huh?' He squinted at her blearily, and she waved her toast at him.

'Whatever it was you went out for yesterday. Group course . . . project . . . thingy, whatsit. You know what I mean.' James snickered, and she flapped her hand at him. 'Shut up, you, it's early. Did you get it done?' she asked Nick.

It took another blank moment before he even remembered the cover story he'd given. 'Oh! Um, yeah. Yeah, it's all finished.'

'Well, good.' She rolled her eyes. 'What time did you get to bed last night? You're barely conscious.'

'Early,' Greg said contemptuously. 'He was asleep way before me!'

'Only because you stayed up an hour past your bedtime,' James chided. 'I'm beginning to think we should move that computer out of your room.'

Greg's face was all affronted dignity. 'Simon's mum lets him stay up till after midnight,' he accused.

'Yes?' their mother said. 'Well, when you move out and go to live in her house, she can set your bedtime too. Rachel, it doesn't matter how slowly you eat that, you're still going to school.'

'But it's gross!' Rachel said, making a face over her cereal bowl.

'You're not supposed to like it, it's good for you. Nick, is your dad feeding you tonight?'

Again he had to struggle to tune back in and figure out what she was talking about. What day was it? Wednesday? So he had football after school. 'Er, yeah, probably.' The lower and upper school teams had their practices together so he and Kyle both played, and their father usually took them out for pizza afterwards.

'All right. What time is this party you're going to?'

He'd forgotten about that too. 'Um ... I'm not sure.'

His mother sighed. 'It's a wonder they make it out of nappies, isn't it?' she remarked to James before turning back to Nick. 'All right. Give me a ring tonight and let me know what you're doing. I can come and pick you up if you need me to. You don't want to be too late. And Nick, at least *try* and find your brain before you get to school this morning, would you?'

In his current state of mind, that was far too much to ask. Nick turned up to school, but afterwards he couldn't have said who he sat with, what they'd studied, or even what lessons he'd been in. He had the second orb in his bag, wrapped up inside his football kit, and he had to keep peering inside to be sure it was safe. He was petrified it would get damaged, but he couldn't leave it stashed at his mum's house because of the way Greg casually pawed through all his stuff. He doubted Mr Grey would look kindly on the 'my little brother broke it' excuse.

He was even more conscious of the bracelet – a visible bulge under the tight-fitting sleeves of his shirt and school jumper. Any jewellery more than stud ear-rings was against the school rules, and things could get very sticky if one of his teachers tried to get him to take it off. Whenever he wasn't writing, Nick tried to keep his right hand hidden away out of view.

Which was why, when the metal suddenly grew blazing hot during afternoon registration, he had it tucked into his trouser pocket.

Miss Newcombe had taken the register and was in the middle of delivering a long and boring lecture. Nick had tuned it out so thoroughly he wasn't sure if it was about exam revision or school uniforms. He was slouched down low in his chair, trying to go as unnoticed as possible.

The scorching heat struck completely without warning. One moment he was contemplating the staples in the nearest wall display, the next he was out of his chair with a startled yell. The class broke into giggles and Miss Newcombe pursed her lips at him impatiently.

'Yes, Nick?'

He squirmed, wanting desperately to shake his hand and swear, but aware of all the eyes on him. He slid his gaze under the desk and blanched at the sight of white light beginning to spill out of his school bag. 'Sorry, miss, er, can I be excused?' he said despairingly.

Neil Sachs whispered something to the boys at his table, and the laughter took a decidedly more spiteful turn.

Miss Newcombe sighed in disapproval. 'Nick, you've just come from lunch. Why couldn't you . . . ?'

He really couldn't stand this for a second longer. 'I'm sorry, miss, I really have to . . .' He grabbed his bag and ran out of the room. The sound of his classmates' amusement followed him all the way down the corridor.

He scrabbled at the buckles of his bag to get the orb out, hissing with relief as his fingers closed around it and the pain and the light went away. With a quick glance over his shoulder to be sure no one had noticed, he raised the ball to peer into the glass.

Below the name and address it now read: *Wednesday 27th February, 3.15 p.m.*

Nick swore.

Three-fifteen? School didn't end till three-thirty. And Goldbrook Avenue was way over the other side of town. Even if he set off jogging as soon as the bell went, he wouldn't get there before four.

He was just going to have to be late.

Registration period wasn't over, but Nick really couldn't face returning to Miss Newcombe's class. Instead he began a slow walk to the science block. If he timed it right, he should get there just as the bell rang.

Before he'd managed a dozen paces, the bracelet began to heat up again.

Nick stopped, and then backtracked. The heat faded out. He tried to move forward again, with the same result.

The bracelet wasn't going to let him go to class. He had an obligation to fulfil, no matter how inconvenient the timing. Heart sinking, he turned and headed for the rear of the school.

As the bell rang for fifth lesson, Nick threaded his way through the crowds that spilled into the corridors. He felt like there must be a flashing neon sign above his head that screamed out, *Bunking!* Any minute now, a teacher would step out in front of him and demand to know where he was going.

But of course nobody did. He was just another kid in the crowd. No one paid any attention at all.

He made it past the side of the school to the back gate. It was guaranteed to be locked, and Nick was about to try and climb over when it occurred to him to try the bracelet. He closed his hand round the padlock, and a moment later there was a loud clunk. The gate moved stiffly thanks to years of disuse, but it was open.

Despite his grim situation, Nick couldn't help but smile to himself a little. Mr Grey's bracelet would be a very cool thing indeed . . . if only he was the one in control of its powers. Or if he just knew how to get the damn thing *off*.

Now that he knew the truth about Mr Grey's shop, he had a sinking feeling there *was* only one way . . . and that was by completing his job.

His nerves would have preferred it if he'd kept to the back streets, but he couldn't risk getting lost and making himself late. It hardly mattered, anyway: even with his tie stuffed away in his pocket he was clearly a schoolboy. But nobody gave him a second glance and he made it to Goldbrook Avenue less than five minutes shy of the appointed time.

The buildings round here were all flats. Small individual blocks rather than monster towers, but definitely rather run-down. The ugly brick buildings were decades old and didn't look like they'd been maintained since they were new. Most of the reachable stretches of blank wall showed signs of a graffiti war between 'Razz' and 'Arbo', and there was shattered glass across several parking spaces.

Nick found flat seventeen listed on the front of one of the buildings. There was an intercom, but it didn't seem to be functional, and someone had propped the main door open with a rolled-up magazine that was turning to mush from the damp. He let himself in and mounted the stairs.

Number seventeen was the middle flat. Nick stood outside its door a moment, and heard the muted buzz of unidentifiable music from within. The bracelet would probably take him through this door if he wanted, but it seemed too invasive to just walk in. He knocked on it left-handed.

He was just raising his hand to knock again when the music cut off. A moment later the door was opened by a tall, narrow-shouldered man with a neat beard and his hair in gelled spikes. Nick put his age somewhere in the early to mid twenties. He was dressed more expensively than his home would suggest – in an embroidered silver shirt and smart trousers. His posture was decidedly wary, and he waited for Nick to speak without offering any prompt.

'Er, Tariq Khalil?' Nick blurted awkwardly.

'Yeah. What's up?' Tariq folded his arms and leaned back against the wall beside the doorframe. Nick caught a glimpse of a long scar that travelled along the back of his hand and up his sleeve. He shifted nervously.

'I'm, er . . . my name is Nick Spencer. I work for Bargains.' He struggled to shove up the multiple layers of coat, jumper and shirt sleeve to display the bracelet.

Tariq's eyebrows lifted at the sight of it. 'Grey's taking work-experience kids now?' he wondered. He took a step backwards. 'Come in.'

He led the way inside. Nick looked around the flat

in a series of quick sideways glances as he followed Tariq. The first room they passed clearly belonged to a girl – young, but judging by the profusion of posters that wouldn't have looked out of place in Rachel's room, probably not young enough to be Tariq's daughter. A sister?

He wasn't sure whether to find that reassuring or not. It was automatically less scary to be collecting from someone who still lived with his parents, but he was unnerved by Tariq's offhand attitude – and his scars. Nick could see another one disappearing under his hair-line as he followed him into the living-dining room.

Curiosity pushed him to speak. 'You know Mr Grey then?' he asked. He found it hard to believe someone would enter into a deal with the shop if they knew its proprietor and what he could do.

'Oh, we go way back.' Tariq smiled wryly. 'You might say I'm . . . paying on the instalment plan.' His gaze drifted down over Nick, assessing. 'But this is the first time he's sent anybody else to collect for him.'

'Well, um, this is kind of a payment plan too,' Nick explained. He grimaced. 'Although it wasn't exactly my choice.'

'It never is.' Tariq flashed him a sympathetic grin, and Nick started to relax a little. 'So, wow, he let you pay off your debt in service to him?' He rested his arms on the back of a chair and leaned forward. 'That's a new one on me. What are the terms?'

'I . . . don't know,' Nick realized, and his stomach squirmed uneasily. When Mr Grey had said he could work off his debt . . . exactly how much work would that take? Five collections? Fifty? Five thousand? How long was he going to be at the mercy of the bracelet that chained him to the shop?

Tariq gave a dark snort. 'Yeah. That *isn't* a new one. Take my advice, mate – get out now, if there's any way you can. It may seem like a reasonable deal at the start, but the more you pay, the less you end up paying for.'

Nick shifted uncomfortably, unsure what to say. Tariq squared up to him and extended his hand. 'Got the ball?'

'Er, yeah.' Nick dug it out of his bag. 'Um, do you need to give me something else?' he said, thinking of Mullen's trophy, and his own sketch. 'Like . . . something of yours to cement the deal?'

'Oh, that'll be taken care of,' Tariq said, with a hint of a grim smile. Nick wasn't sure he wanted to know what he was talking about. If he'd known in advance what would happen with Mullen, would he still have been able to shake the guy's hand?

He held the orb in a loose grip and dithered. 'All right, then, I guess . . .'

Tariq shrugged easily. 'Go for it.'

Nick accepted his long-fingered hand and gave it a single firm shake.

The bracelet tightened and energy crackled. He was halfway ready for it this time and he didn't quite stagger, but he still gritted his teeth hard enough to make his jaw ache. The world around him warped, and then stabilized. When it did, the orb in his left hand had turned milky white.

Tariq flinched, and a dark line appeared slashed across the front of his shirt. Nick didn't understand it at first – until the line started spreading, and he realized it was blood.

'Jesus! Are you all right?' He started forward with no real clue what to do. What the hell had he just done?

'Yeah. Fine.' Tariq waved him back and undid the top few buttons of his shirt to lift it over his head. A long narrow strip of skin had been torn away across his chest. The cut lay over a criss-cross of similar scars – all over his chest, his back, his arms and his stomach. Nick paled, but Tariq just prodded the new wound and hissed a little like it was no more than a nasty paper cut.

'You'd think one day I would learn not to wear my nice shirts,' he observed to himself, shaking his head. He wadded the shirt into a ball and walked over to open the bathroom door and stuff it in the laundry basket.

'Bloody *hell*!' Nick followed him, still stunned. 'Wh-what was that?'

'Pain.' Tariq smiled tightly as he picked up a towel. 'I take it. Other people get to be free of it. It's always in demand.'

'You're selling *pain*?' he said, bewildered.

Tariq patted his chest with the towel, grimacing. 'Technically I'm selling the *absence* of pain,' he clarified. 'Which means I get to have some. Not a lot, but . . . it adds up.' He contemplated his scars in the mirror.

'That . . . doesn't sound like such a great deal,' Nick said, unable to drag his eyes away from the lines that scored Tariq's skin.

Tariq turned to face him, draping the towel over his shoulder. He smiled tightly. 'Mr Grey doesn't give great deals.' He sighed and tilted his head back, silent for a moment, then looked at Nick. 'I started doing this to save my sister,' he said. 'She was ill – she was dying – and it was happening too fast for the doctors to even figure out why it was happening. So I started paying Grey my flesh and blood to keep her alive.' He shook his head.

'And then they *did* figure it out, and she got better. Only I'm still paying. Because that was the bargain I made, you see. Grey didn't agree to protect her from the illness for as long as I paid him; he agreed to *keep her alive*. If I fail to keep up the payments, then she'll die.'

Nick felt sick – and not just because of the obvious. If the bracelet hadn't prevented him returning to his lessons, he would have shown up for this meeting nearly an hour late.

Long enough for Tariq's sister to die because of his tardiness?

Tariq showed his teeth in a humourless grin. 'Yeah,' he said. 'That's how Mr Grey operates. Whatever you think you're working for, you're not going to get it. Not the way you want, and not without paying more than you can afford. You don't want to waste your time trying to come out ahead. You just need to get out, full stop.'

Nick bit his lip in dismay. 'But how am I meant to do that?' he said. He couldn't imagine Grey letting him out of their agreement just because he asked nicely.

Tariq gave a bitter laugh. 'Oh, trust me, if I knew the answer to that, you wouldn't be talking to me now.'

It wasn't a reply that gave Nick a great deal of confidence.

As Nick made his way back towards town, the bag on his shoulder seemed to grow steadily heavier. It was bulked out twice as much as usual by his football kit, the boots nudging him in the side every step of the way.

His football kit. Nick stopped and swore. He was supposed to have football after school today, which was – he checked his watch – pretty much right *now*. He couldn't just skip it, either, because Kyle would be there and their dad was meant to be picking them both up after practice.

He swore again, and broke into a shambling run.

By the time he'd fought his way back through the throng of school kids moving in the opposite direction, he'd missed the first half-hour of the session. Mr Reynolds hailed him from the school field. 'Hey! Spencer! What time do you call this?'

Nick winced. 'Sorry, sir!' he called back. 'I forgot we had practice!'

'Well, hurry up and get your kit on, and give me two laps of the field. Your brother managed to make it here without anyone to hold his hand.' From behind the teacher, Kyle sent him a smirk and a two-fingered salute.

Nick limped over to the empty changing rooms. Being late did have one good side: there was no one around to get a look at the bracelet as he swapped his white shirt for the crumpled blue PE top. But he was still exhausted from his flat-out sprint, and the sweat from his exertion soon turned icy in the cold air. He did his laps of the field at a miserable stagger as Mr Reynolds shouted sadistic encouragements.

'Gutted,' Peter Price said as Nick finally joined the rest of the boys.

'Oi, where were you in science?' Rob Wiggan

asked. Damn. He'd forgotten Rob was in his group.

'I was there,' Nick lied, blowing on his hands to try and warm his fingers.

'I didn't see you.'

'Well, you're blind, aren't you?' Peter mocked him. 'Are you going to fetch that ball or what?'

Fortunately, that was all the interrogation he got, and Kyle was out of hearing range when it happened. He didn't need his half-brother finding out he'd been bunking on top of everything else.

Nick was completely useless for the rest of the practice, but nobody found that unusual. He was a reserve for the upper-school team, and not a very good one. He really only kept going to football because Kyle did, and the school was starved of people willing to give up Wednesday afternoons. Most of the players huddled around stamping their feet to keep warm while Kyle and a few other enthusiasts did the running around.

'That was pathetic,' Mr Reynolds informed them all at the end of the session. 'You can *all* give me a lap of the field before you get changed. And, Nick, if you're late again, you can do ten next time.'

'Yes, sir,' they all groaned, and Nick forced himself to stagger round the field again. When they got back to the changing rooms, he slumped on the bench, reluctant to move.

'Come on, hurry up,' Kyle said, his hair standing up in all directions as he pulled the PE top over his head. 'I'm starving!'

'Yeah, just give me a second.' He stood up wearily and started to peel off his own top. No, wait, he couldn't do that. He swore internally, for a moment too numbed by tiredness to figure out what to do next. Finally he pulled his school shirt back on over the PE top and started to button it up.

'Ugh, that's *mank*,' Kyle said. He whipped out his can of deodorant and sprayed Nick with it liberally. 'I have to share a car with you!'

'Get lost,' Nick protested, coughing in the toxic cloud. 'I'll change when we get home.'

'You're gross,' Kyle said, and proceeded to spray himself with almost as much deodorant as he'd used on Nick.

Nick changed out of his shorts, but didn't bother with his tie or his school shoes. There wouldn't be many teachers around anyway. Normally he was paranoid about all the little rules that his schoolmates couldn't be bothered with, but today it seemed stupid and trivial. What was the threat of detention against the things that Mr Grey held over him?

Putting on his coat, he looked at his phone and found a message from Katie on his voice mail. 'Oi, Nicky, I don't know where you went in science, but you'd better not have forgotten about tonight. We're meeting at my house; Sunita's brother's going to drive us. He's picking us up between half six and seven.'

Nick swore as he lowered the phone. He *had* forgotten about the party – even after his mum had reminded him this morning. He was going to have to go there pretty much straight after dinner. There would be no time to take Tariq's orb back to the shop.

He groped in his bag to be sure it was still safe. Was it his imagination, or did he feel a little buzz of static from the concealed bracelet as he touched it?

He didn't like the idea of carrying the thing around for hours, but it wasn't as if he had any choice. He wasn't on a fixed time limit for *returning* the orbs – and surely Mr Grey had to understand that Nick had other commitments . . .

. . . Didn't he?

Nick couldn't help but think that 'understanding' wasn't a word that went very well with his mental picture of the shopkeeper.

'Come *on*,' Kyle groaned from where he was messing with his hair in front of the mirror. They were the last ones left in the changing rooms. 'What are you doing? Dad's probably gone home by now.'

'All right, I'm coming! Keep your knickers on,' Nick grumbled. He swung his bag over his shoulder and followed Kyle out.

They stopped briefly at his dad's house to change their clothes and dump their stuff. Fortunately, Nick had the excuse of going back to his mum's afterwards for keeping his school bag with him. But the limited stock of clothes he kept at his dad's was running low, so he struggled to find an outfit that was both concealing *and* not too socially embarrassing. In the end he chose a blue-and-black-striped shirt that was more loose-fitting than he would have liked and threw a big coat on over it.

'Do you want to put your bag in the boot?' his dad said as they went back out to the car.

'No, it's OK. I'll keep it.' He winced at the thought of it bouncing around as they drove.

'Come on! I'm starving,' Kyle said. His clothes were probably more suitable for a party than Nick's; he was all in black as usual, with a sleeveless band T-shirt, silver rings and a black cord necklace. Someone with Kyle's fashion sense could have worn the bracelet openly without anybody even noticing. On Nick, however, it would have stood out as painfully uncharacteristic.

'What do you boys want to eat?' their dad asked, more a ritual than a true question.

'Pizza!' Kyle insisted gleefully, but Nick just shrugged. His father gave him a sidelong glance as he pulled out from the kerb.

'You feeling all right, Nick?'

He made an effort to smile. 'Yeah. I'm just a bit tired.' *Drained* might be a better word. He'd been rigid with tension all day, and running back from Tariq's and then around the field without a proper warm-up hadn't exactly relaxed his muscles.

'You're going out tonight, aren't you?' his dad asked.

'Where?' Kyle demanded, sitting forward.

'Katie's friend Daz's party,' Nick answered. Just the thought of it was giving him a headache. He wished there was some way he could think of to get out of it.

'Oh.' Kyle quickly lost interest. 'Dad, did I tell you I won the story competition in English?'

'No.' Their father glanced at him in the rear-view mirror. 'That's pretty good.'

'Yeah. And Mrs Wilkins said I could be a writer. I want to start my own webcomic. I've been working on a script for it. Nick can do the illustrations.'

'I don't have time,' Nick said sourly.

'I don't mean now, I mean over the summer,' Kyle said, rolling his eyes.

'I'm going to be *busy* then,' he snapped. 'I've got college coming up and everything.' And there was no guarantee he would have his art skills back by then. A chill slid down his spine at the thought. What was he going to do if Grey didn't come through on their deal before the GCSEs?

What was he going to do if Grey didn't come through at all?

His father frowned at him, but didn't say anything. 'Why don't you illustrate it yourself, Kyle?' he suggested instead.

'Because it'll look *pants*,' Kyle said. 'Oh, come on, Nick, I need you to help me. You'll get fifty per cent of the profits!'

'Oh, this is a money-making venture now?' Their father chuckled.

Kyle kept on pushing and pushing. 'Come on, Nick. It's good advertising! Loads of people from all over the world would get to see your artwork. At least help me design the characters!'

'Just give it a rest, OK?' Nick massaged his forehead with his fingers. 'I've got a headache.' He laid his head back against the seat for the remainder of the journey and kept his eyes closed.

He only picked at his meal in the restaurant. He felt feverish, and today his favourite pizza just tasted like mushy cardboard. He felt more bloated and sick with every bite.

Was Tariq right? Was Mr Grey just playing with

him, dangling the possibility of salvation before him but never planning to deliver it?

Nick stared down at his hands. They seemed like alien prosthetics to him now; unfamiliar, useless. What was he going to do if he didn't get his art skills back? Every plan he'd made for the future hinged on him being able to draw. He'd never been any good at anything else.

Was it even possible to relearn the skills he'd lost? The part of his brain that controlled them might be gone. He could practise for years and years and never get beyond aimless scribbles. Would he have to just accept that? *Could* he accept it? Give up on ever being an artist – hell, give up on even scrawling a useful map if somebody asked him for directions? Fail his art and graphics GCSEs, and drop some grades in most of the others for missing out diagrams? Forget about going to college this year – if ever?

And then start a new life, doing . . . what?

Working as an unpaid slave for Mr Grey, probably. He took a sip of Coke to try and cut through the sick feeling clogging the back of his throat.

'You sure you're up to this party tonight?' his father asked. 'You don't look at all well.'

Nick was pretty sure he wasn't up to anything – but he couldn't face Katie hassling him about it afterwards either. Maybe he could just show up for an hour or so and then leave early. He managed a tight smile. 'I'm OK,' he said. 'I'm just a bit knackered after football. I'll be all right once I've had a rest.'

There was nothing that his dad could do to help him anyway.

Nick's father dropped him off outside Katie's. There was no chance to make an escape; she opened the front door even as he was getting out of the car.

'Hi.' She let him in and quickly closed the door behind him, shivering in her glittery top. 'I was wondering if you were coming. Where'd you go last lesson? I was waiting for you in science.'

'Sorry. I was in the sickbay again,' he lied. 'I had another headache.'

'Yeah, right,' she said, but her mother came out before she could question him further.

'Oh, hi, Nick. What time are you two leaving?'

'Sunita's brother's picking us up,' Katie said. She moved to the porch window and peered out. 'I think this might be him now, actually. He's just turning the car round.'

'All right. You two have fun,' her mum said. 'And make sure you ring me if you need a lift back. I don't want you walking home on your own.'

'I will,' Katie promised. She glanced at Nick. 'Do you want to dump your bag here? You can pick it up after.'

'No, that's OK.' He didn't dare risk leaving the orb unattended, especially now the collection was made. What would Mr Grey do to him if he lost it?

'Let's go then,' she said, opening the door just as a car horn honked. 'Bye, Mum.' She nudged Nick in the side as they walked up the drive. 'And stop looking like I'm making you eat Brussels sprouts. This is going to be fun, I promise.'

Somehow, Nick couldn't quite believe her.

He never had liked parties.

This one was supposedly in honour of Katie's

bandmate Daz, although his actual birthday had been a couple of weeks ago. It was mostly an excuse to cram a load of people into Daz's tiny house so they could all get drunk and dance. He supposed it would have been more fun if he actually drank. Or danced.

The house was hot, and it thronged with people. He knew he'd look like an idiot if he didn't dump his coat and bag in the bedrooms like everyone else. He wedged his bag in the most protected corner he could find, but he was haunted by the image of some drunk guy coming in to look for his coat in the heap and just casually *kicking* . . . Every clink of glass bottles from the kitchen made him flinch.

He knew hardly any of the people at the party. Daz, the bass player in Katie's band, was two years older, and Nick only vaguely recognized most of his mates from when they'd attended his school a couple of years back. Aside from Katie, the guests he did know were casual acquaintances he might say hi to, not stand and chat with. He drank way more glasses of Coke than he really wanted and spent a lot of time lurking in a corner, pretending to nod along to songs that he didn't actually know that well.

Just like every party he'd ever been to, really, only with the added crushing pressure of his bargain with Grey hanging over him. Every second that he wasted here was one more for Mr Grey to get angry, one more chance for the orb to get damaged or the bracelet to be exposed.

'Nick!' Katie approached him, grinning giddily. 'You owe me a dance.' She grabbed his free hand and tried to haul him away from the wall.

He pressed his shoulders more firmly back against it. 'I don't dance,' he reminded her.

'Oh, come on!' She tried again to shift him. 'Look at Eric – he's dancing, and he looks like a rubber chicken on a string. No one *cares* that you're not any good at it.'

'*I* care. I don't want to.'

'Don't be such a wimp. One dance. Not even to anything embarrassing! Come on.' Katie pulled at him with both hands, and almost fell over backwards as he braced himself in the corner. She spluttered with laughter as she tried to regain her balance. 'Aargh! Help me, I'm falling!' She grabbed him by the arm to haul herself back up. 'Ow! Jesus – are you wearing armour or something under there? I think I just broke a nail.'

She groped out the shape of the bracelet under his sleeve, and pushed back his cuff to get a look at it. 'Oh, what's this?'

Nick pulled his arm away and hastily covered it up, stomach churning even though he knew it was just a piece of fancy jewellery to anybody else. 'Do you mind?'

'Not particularly, no,' she said cheerfully, grabbing his arm again and peering up the sleeve. 'Wow, cool bracelet! Why are you wearing a long-sleeved shirt over it, you dork? You should be showing it off.'

He shrugged uncomfortably, but Katie refused to lose interest.

'Can I try it on?' She prised at the metal band which, of course, got her nowhere. 'Damn, that's tight,' she said, inspecting her nails for damage. 'What did you do, have it specially adjusted to fit you or something? Where did you get it from?'

'A shop,' he said shortly; there was no other option. He tried to slip his hand back into his pocket, but Katie wouldn't let him.

'No, let me have another look.' She twisted his arm until he was forced to let her inspect it more closely. 'This must have cost you a packet. Seriously, where'd you get it?' To his discomfort, she traced her fingers over the eye symbol. 'I could swear I've seen that pattern somewhere before.'

'Seriously?' He stared at her. 'Where?'

He must have been too frantic, because she scrunched her eyebrows up in a frown. 'I don't know,' she said slowly, scrutinizing his face. 'Nick, what . . . ?'

'I've got to get some air,' he said abruptly, unable to face the prospect of probing questions. 'I'm going to get my coat.' He bolted for the stairs.

Katie followed him up. 'Where're you going, Nicky?' she asked with one hand on her hip as he dug for his bag and coat in the heap. 'We've only been here an hour and a half.'

To Nick it felt more like ten or twelve.

'I'm going home.' He knew he sounded like a whiny little kid, but he couldn't keep the tone out of his voice. 'I don't feel well.' He found his coat, but his bag wasn't in the corner where he'd left it. He stood back to scan the room, his heart racing. What if someone else had taken it by mistake?

'Oh, give it a rest,' Katie said. 'You've been saying that all week whenever you don't want to talk to me.'

'Yeah, well, maybe you should take a bloody hint!' Nick finally spotted his bag, which some idiot had slung onto the bed. He grabbed it and clutched it against his chest, praying the orb hadn't been damaged when it was thrown around.

'I'm going home,' he repeated. 'Tell Daz I'm sorry. If he even remembers who I am.'

What the hell was he doing at this stupid party? He was risking his entire future to be somewhere that he didn't even want to be.

'I'll see you tomorrow,' he said, and jogged down the stairs, pulling on his coat as he went.

It was a relief to be out of the house. It was pitch black and bitterly cold outside, the air slicing through him, but even that felt good after the oppressive crowding of the party.

Daz's house was in a part of town Nick didn't know well, but the blaze of streetlights made it easy for him to find his way down towards the town centre. He was almost alone on the quiet streets, his footsteps echoing and his breath preceding him in clouds of misty white.

The roads around the town were still busy, but the pedestrian precinct was dead. The occasional pockets of light and activity made him feel more isolated, not less. His trepidation grew as he made his way down the back alley towards Bargains. The door opened under his touch, but all the lights were off and he had to make his way down to the orb room by touch. Was the shop even open at this time of night? Or did Grey just leave his door unlocked, relying on other, more deadly, security measures to take care of unwanted intruders?

Nick swallowed, but kept going.

The orb room was lit, but not in any natural manner. The orbs themselves gave off a faint silvery glow, as cold and unfriendly as hospital lights. It killed what little night vision he had without trading it for true illumination.

If he'd thought this place was creepy in the daytime, it had nothing on the spiders of fear that were crawling over his skin right now.

'You are *late*, Mr Spencer,' Mr Grey said from behind him. Nick flinched away, and the bag over his shoulder scraped along the edge of one of the shelves. His heart froze solid in his chest until the sound of rocking glass finally came to a halt.

'I know, I-I-I'm sorry,' he stammered. 'I couldn't get away . . .'

'I do not need a tardy employee,' the shopkeeper said. In the silver glow of the orbs, his dark eyes looked like pools of mercury. 'I do not need a *clumsy* employee. If you are not prepared to take your contract seriously, perhaps now is the time to terminate it.'

Nick didn't see him do anything, but on the word 'terminate', the bracelet vibrated warningly around his wrist. He wasn't sure they were talking about just being fired. He swallowed hard. 'No, I'll . . . I'll do better,' he rasped. He scrambled to get Tariq's orb from his bag. 'It won't happen again.'

'It had better not.' Grey plucked the orb from his fumbling fingers and studied it with a predatory eye. 'Your next collection is in my office. Take it now, and don't try my patience again.'

'Yes, sir.' Nick swallowed, and shuffled down the darkened hallway towards the office. There was no light switch anywhere that he could find, and he didn't have the nerve to ask the shopkeeper to turn on the lights. He overshot the office door at first, and almost fell down the stairs before he realized his mistake and backtracked. He groped for the door handle and pushed it open.

It was dark. A soft scratching noise made his heart stand still, until he realized it was the hands of the clock turning. He almost tripped over one of the chests on his way in, and winced as its contents clinked ominously.

The orb on the desk didn't glow. Nick had to feel around the desktop with great care to find his next collection. He tried not to guess what stolen dream it represented, or how many more like it he would have to collect before Grey pronounced them even.

If he ever did. Tariq had said Mr Grey would never let him go. That the 'deal' was no more than a scam. But what choice did he have? The shopkeeper held Nick's future in the palm of his hand – and Nick's *life* was held in the shackle around his own wrist. One wrong move, and he might end up with worse problems than just being fired.

And no one would know what had happened to him. All of a sudden, he was freshly aware that Grey was the only one who even knew where Nick was. The darkened shop seemed to close in around him like a tomb as he stumbled back out to the orb room.

The shopkeeper had once again vanished. Had he actually *gone*? Or was he still lurking in the shadows, watching Nick's every move? Nick scurried away down the corridor with undue haste. The panic didn't leave him as he escaped and sprinted for the relative safety of the streets outside – only to rear back in terror as a shadow blocked the mouth of the alley.

Then the silhouetted figure spoke. 'OK, Nicky. I think it's about time you and I had a talk.'

'Y'ou're a prat,' Katie said as they walked out past the shut-up Westfield Centre. 'What? You thought I wasn't going to follow you?'

Nick gave a noncommittal shrug and didn't say anything.

She jerked her thumb towards the alley. 'So what were you doing down there that was so important? And it better not involve buying drugs, because believe me, I don't have the patience to deal with that much stupidity.'

'Do I *look* like I've been buying drugs?' Nick asked sullenly, stuffing his hands in his pockets.

'Well, right now you look like you're *on* them,' she said. She gave him a sideways glance. 'Seriously, the way you've been the past couple of days you might as well change your name to Deadhead McZombie. Did you think I wouldn't notice?'

'It's got nothing to do with you!'

'No, I didn't think it did. Not the point, Nicholas.' Katie raised her eyebrows expectantly.

'Can't you just stay out of it?' he demanded.

'No, I'm a nosy cow,' she said easily. 'And you know you've never, ever been able to keep a secret from me, so you might as well give it up.'

Nick closed his eyes in despair. 'It's not a *game*, Katie.'

She flicked her hair back from her face. 'Yeah. The sneaking off to midnight meetings in dark alleys was a little bit of a clue there.'

'It's nowhere near midnight,' he corrected peevishly.

'And this is a good place to hang out at any time of night?' she said, with a pointed look at the drunks outside the trio of pubs on the corner. 'You can't go running off this time, because I am *not* walking home on my own from here.'

'I didn't ask you to follow me.' Nick hunched his shoulders.

'Well, you didn't exactly give me much choice! If you would actually *talk* to me—'

'I can't!' he burst out. He stopped walking and gave a slow sigh, rubbing his hands over his face. 'You wouldn't believe me if I told you, OK?' he said in calmer tones. 'It sounds crazy – it *is* crazy – and there's nothing you can do to help, so there's no point in me even telling you.'

'How about you let me decide what I will and won't believe, OK?' Katie said, sounding just as frustrated as he was. 'There is *nothing* you can tell me that is half as wacko as the stuff I'm coming up with in my head already.'

Nick let out a bitter laugh, tilting his head back to look at the overcast sky. How the hell had this ever become his *life*?

'Fine,' he said despairingly. 'Fine! You want to know what's going on?' He whirled to face her. 'I'm being blackmailed into working for an evil bastard with magical powers. He's taken away my ability to draw, and he won't give it back unless I do what he says. Oh, yeah, and he's got me hooked up to a shock bracelet to make sure I don't welsh on the deal.' He yanked back his coat sleeve to expose the metal band. 'Any helpful suggestions?'

Katie blinked at him in the orange glow of the streetlights.

'OK, that's a *little* more nuts than I was prepared for,' she admitted after a moment. 'How about we try this from the beginning?'

So he told her the whole story. It seemed kind of pointless not to; it wasn't as if she could think he was any *more* crazy at this point. The words tumbled out more easily than he was expecting: it was a relief to just share it with *someone*, no matter what she might think of it. He didn't look at Katie while he was talking, and she stayed atypically silent. When he'd run out of words, he just started walking again, his eyes on the streams of headlights moving in the distance.

There was a long, contemplative pause. 'Well,' Katie said finally, catching him up, '*that* sounds like a load of balls.'

It was hard to protest against that assessment. Nick

shrugged his shoulders, still looking straight ahead. 'Uh-huh.'

'*But*,' she continued, 'since I know for a fact you're the crappiest liar on Earth, I know *you* believe it. Nicky, my friend, someone is having you on. You've been hypnotized or something.'

'I wish,' he said resignedly. He knew deep down in his gut that everything he'd seen was real. It was too clear and crisp and intense to think otherwise.

'You have,' Katie insisted as they turned into her street. 'Either they're filming you for some hidden-camera thing or you've stumbled into the world's weirdest role-playing game. You've been hypnotized into believing you've forgotten how to draw, they keep giving you shocks through the bracelet, and that's got you worked up to a point where you'll accept anything they throw at you. It's classic mind-control stuff. The power of suggestion and all that.'

Nick shook his head. 'It's more than that. Trust me.'

'I just wish I knew where I'd seen that eye symbol before,' Katie mused, not listening to him. 'Let me have another look at the bracelet.'

She pulled him over to stand in the halo from the nearest streetlight and bent his arm at an awkward angle to inspect the piece of jewellery.

'I definitely, definitely know that from somewhere,' she insisted, chewing her lip. She straightened up. 'I'll tell you what. I'll try to work that out tonight, and then tomorrow we'll see what we can do about getting you deprogrammed. There's got to be someone who can do it.'

It was easier to just agree than try and argue further. 'All right,' he said with a faint sigh as they reached the end of her drive. 'I'll see you tomorrow then.'

'Yeah.' She gave him a light slap on the arm. 'Hang in there. This Grey bloke can't get away with this. We'll figure out what he's done to you, and then we'll sue his arse off. You'll be rich.'

'Yeah.' He gave a plastic smile.

If only he really believed it would be anywhere near that simple.

Nick strode back to his mum's house in an increasingly dark mood. He knew he should probably be grateful Katie didn't just think he was nuts, but instead he was irrationally frustrated. Why couldn't she just *believe* him? Her scepticism would only put them both in danger. He purposely hadn't told her exactly where to find the shop, but she'd seen him come out of the alley. What if she went marching in there to demand that Grey stop messing with Nick's head . . . ?

He stomped through the front door, closing it with a slam. His stepfather appeared in the hall from the living-room doorway.

'Oh, hi, Nick. How was the party?'

'Awful,' Nick said flatly.

James smiled uncertainly. 'Not your kind of thing, huh?' He ran a hand through his thinning blond hair. 'Yeah, I never liked parties much when I was a teenager. I'd much rather have been home with a book.' He gestured over his shoulder. 'I don't know how much you've had to eat, but there's some chocolate in the kitchen if you want some.'

'No thanks,' Nick said gruffly. 'I'm just going to go to bed.'

Greg was on the computer, of course, when he got

up to his room. 'Oi, Nick.' Greg spun halfway round in his swivel chair. 'Want to see the new level I just unlocked? It's really cool. You've got all these demons coming up through these lava cracks in the floor, and if you get too close to them, you catch fire. Come on, let me just save this and I'll show you. You've got to see it, it's hilarious.'

'No.' Nick tossed the box from the game off his bed and onto Greg's. 'Turn the sound off. I'm going to bed.'

'Dick,' Greg said, then turned the volume up higher.

Nick slept poorly that night, even after Greg had traded machine-gun noises for throaty snores. His dreams were a confused mess of dark rainy streets and Mr Grey's almost-black eyes peering at him out of mirrors and shop windows. When he woke, the images drained away like water out of cupped hands, but the unsettled feeling remained.

He had no idea what he was going to do about Katie. As long as she was convinced that his debt to the shop was some kind of scam, she was likely to get them both in trouble. She was sure to keep pushing for him to do something – or worse, try to take matters into her own hands.

Sure enough, she was there to ambush him almost as soon as he walked through the school gates. 'I found it!' she said triumphantly, brandishing a folded-up square of blue paper.

Nick frowned in bewilderment as he took it. 'Found what?'

He unfolded the paper. There were several sheets stapled together, filled on both sides with cramped photocopied printing. The front page was entitled *Secrets and Mysteries*, though whether that was the heading of an article or the name of the publication he couldn't tell. The lower right corner featured a fairly poor drawing of a raven, and the automatic thought, *I could do better than that*, crossed his mind before he remembered that it wasn't true. He crumpled the paper a little in his hands.

'It's this thing they publish up at the university,' Katie said. 'Daz saved it for me a while back because he thought I'd like the ghost candles. Check them out, they're cool. But anyway, look at the back page.'

Nick turned the paper over to discover that *Secrets and Mysteries* had its own classified ads. In amongst the pagans seeking others to practise rituals with, fortune-telling courses and people selling magical paraphernalia, one particular advertisement stood out. It was bounded by a stark, black border and, in discreet small capitals, read:

BARGAINS

13 SPARROW'S WALK

WE CAN SUPPLY YOU WITH ANYTHING YOU WANT

Beneath the words was an intricate rendering of the eye-within-a-star-within-a-knot design that adorned the bracelet on his wrist and the wooden chests in Mr Grey's office. Nick had a feeling that symbol was the *real* message – for anyone with the understanding to read it. He wondered with a chill if there were shops like this all over the country – all over the *world* – advertised in scrappy little publications like this where no one would look twice unless they knew what they were looking for.

'Told you I'd seen that symbol before,' Katie said

triumphantly. 'Do you think it's the logo of a role-playing game or something?' she went on as they crossed the car park. 'Maybe it's some kind of thing where there're clues in the newspapers or on the net to tell people where to turn up, and when they do they're supposed to stay in character all the time. Maybe you said or did something in front of this bloke Grey that made him think you were a player.'

'This is not a game, Katie . . .' Nick said, his words trailing away as his eyes were caught by another listing further down the page. Like the one for Bargains, this advert hardly seemed to even try and explain what it was selling. It said:

TRAPPED IN A BAD DEAL?
DON'T KNOW WHICH WAY TO TURN?
CALL FOR ADVICE AND ASSISTANCE.
NO OBLIGATIONS AGREED WITHOUT YOUR
EXPLICIT CONSENT.

He might have thought it was a misplaced ad for a financial firm had it not been for the fact that it too featured a symbol underneath the text – a stylized sketch of a smoke-filled orb held in cupped hands. Surely *that* couldn't be a coincidence.

'What?' Katie peered over his shoulder.

'Look at this.' He pointed out the second ad to her. The small print at the bottom said it had been placed by an Alfred Cavanagh. There was no address, but there was a mobile phone number.

Katie lifted her eyebrows. 'You think he's involved in this too?'

Nick drew out his own phone and gazed at it uncertainly. 'I don't know.'

'Want me to call him for you?' She made a grab for the mobile, and he hastily yanked it away.

'No, I'll, um . . . I should probably do it myself.' The last thing he needed was for Katie to barge in and try to investigate things on her own. If *he* didn't call this Cavanagh guy, she'd probably do it herself – and if he really was someone who could help Nick, her conviction it was a hoax could ruin everything.

'I'll do it myself,' Nick repeated. He punched in the numbers and raised the phone to his ear. As it started to ring, he couldn't help but wonder if he was doing something very stupid.

XIII

Nick's nerves churned harder with every ring that went unanswered. What was he thinking, calling some random bloke out of the blue? What was he meant to *say*? 'Help me, an evil shopkeeper has stolen my art skills'? The man was going to think he was nuts.

He fished desperately for a way to start the conversation that wouldn't make him sound like a complete wacko. But before he could come up with one, the ringing stopped. He didn't get a response or even voice mail, just a dead line. Nick pulled the phone away from his ear and swore.

'No answer?' Katie asked.

Nick frowned down at his mobile. 'Got cut off.'

'Try it again.' She grabbed it out of his hands and hit redial.

'Katie!' he protested, but she just waved the ringing phone in his face until he took it back. He lifted it to his ear again . . . in time to hear the exact same thing happen. He shook his head in confusion. 'He keeps hanging up on me without even answering.'

'Maybe he's driving,' Katie said. 'It's not nine o'clock yet. He's probably on his way to work.'

'Yeah.' But Nick's stomach tensed anyway. He'd been stupid to think that he'd found a solution. Some complete stranger with a cryptic advertisement wasn't going to be his salvation. There was no way it could be that easy.

He slouched along to registration in a deep depression.

He might as well not have turned up at all. He got his name down on the register, but that was about all that could be said. He couldn't concentrate on anything in history: the teacher's voice droned in his ears, and the words of the textbook turned to alphabet soup. The half-hearted sentences that he scribbled down were barely coherent, let alone on-topic. When he hit the part where he was supposed to draw a diagram, he gave up entirely, and sat in hot-eyed, sullen silence. The teacher was too busy trying to control the noisier members of the class to notice.

His second lesson of the day was science, which promised to be more of the same. As he sat down next to Katie at the front of the class, Mrs Naples dropped his exercise book in front of him.

'Where were you yesterday afternoon, Nick?' she asked. 'You were in school in the morning.'

He panicked. 'Oh, I, um . . . sorry, miss. I was really ill. I had to go home.'

'He had diarrhoea!' Neil Sachs stage whispered from the bench behind. Everyone within earshot broke into laughter, while Mrs Naples did the usual teacher thing of pretending not to hear.

'All right.' Fortunately, Nick bunking off was apparently so unlikely she wasn't going to bother checking his story. 'Just make sure you catch up on what you missed. Oh, and take another look at

Tuesday's work, would you? You were supposed to copy the diagrams out as well.'

'Oh, right. Sorry, miss.' He opened his exercise book and pretended to focus on the red-penned comments until she went away.

Katie leaned over and poked him in the side. 'You seriously can't draw?' she said incredulously.

'No!' Nick opened the book to the back and slashed out the shape of a stick figure. It looked like a four-year-old had drawn it, all broken lines and mismatched proportions. 'That's literally the best I can do.'

'That is so weird,' Katie said, absent-mindedly adding glasses and a moustache to his misshapen creation. She glanced at him. 'Did you call that bloke again?'

Nick shook his head as he scraped his chair in closer to the lab bench. 'No. And I'm not going to. It was a bad idea. He probably doesn't have anything to do with this.'

She rolled her eyes at him. 'Come on, Nick, you've got to . . .' She trailed off as she looked past him over the rest of the class. 'What the *hell* . . . ?'

He twisted round to follow her gaze.

The rest of the room had turned sort of . . . foggy – although that wasn't quite the right word, because there wasn't any mist, just a strange thickness to the air. Their teacher and classmates seemed to be suspended in time. If they were moving at all, it was no more than a millimetre a minute. The background noise was gone, replaced by the dull, muffled feeling of having blocked-up ears. In the next seat, Rob Wiggan was no further away from Nick than Katie was, and yet there was a sense of distance, as if Nick could reach and reach but never quite get close enough to touch him.

Katie leaned past Nick to wave a hand under Rob's nose. 'Oi! Robert. Hello?' He didn't react to the movement, or the piercing whistle she followed it up with.

Neither did anyone else. Nick looked out of the windows and saw that the sky seemed dimmer, and the football players on the field were all moving with glacial slowness.

He and Katie stared at each other.

'Is this something to do with your bracelet?' she asked in a small voice.

Nick shook his head, feeling a chill in his veins. 'No. This isn't me.' They both turned as the classroom door creaked open behind them.

For a heartbeat, Nick was convinced it was Mr Grey. But the man at the door was no one he'd seen before. He was stick-thin, dressed in nondescript black, with longish dark hair and an intense expression. Around his neck he wore an ornate-looking pendant in the shape of metal hands clasped around a dark, round crystal.

He zeroed in immediately on Nick and Katie – not hard, Nick supposed, since they were the only ones not affected by whatever had immobilized the rest of the world.

'You called?' he said.

Nick finally got it. 'You're Cavanagh,' he blurted out.

The man inclined his head in a brief nod. Somehow, he'd been able to locate them after they'd dialled his number. More than that, he'd even known which two people touched the phone and had cast this spell to include them.

Katie got to her feet warily. 'You did this to them?' She indicated the rest of the class.

Cavanagh gave a smile that transformed the sharp lines of his face into something much more charismatic. 'I didn't do anything to them,' he said. 'I did something to us. It's the only way we can meet without attracting the attention of Edmund Grey. Which, I assume, is why you called me.' He regarded the two of them with cool, green eyes.

'Er, yeah.' Nick stood too, and clumsily drew his layers of sleeves back from the bracelet. 'I was hoping you could help me with . . . this.'

Cavanagh's mouth opened slightly at the sight of it, and he muttered a word that Nick didn't understand. 'If that's what it looks like . . .' He sat down abruptly on the edge of Mrs Naples's desk. 'This is quite a departure from Grey's usual games. I'm going to need you to tell me everything.'

Katie was still staring around with the same kind of wide-eyed shock Nick must have worn when he saw Mullen's muscles disappear. 'Can they see us?' she asked.

Cavanagh gave a faint shrug. 'Yes and no. We're in a kind of . . . bubble, if you like.' His hand briefly touched the pendant around his neck. 'Time is passing both inside and out of this bubble, but for the duration of the illusion they just . . . won't notice us. When it ends, they'll think you've been sitting in your seats doing ordinary things all along. It's not all that clever a trick – you're just fooling people into seeing what they expect to see.'

He might not be that impressed with it, but Nick's heart was beating fast in his chest. It was the first demonstration of magical power he'd seen that hadn't come directly from Mr Grey. The first flicker of hope that maybe, just maybe, there could be a way out of this that didn't involve playing Grey's game for ever.

'Can you break his . . . enchantments?' he asked, hesitating for a fraction over the final word. It sounded crazy, and yet what else could you call it but *magic*?

'Grey's strong,' Cavanagh said. 'Too strong for anybody to battle head on. But that doesn't mean he's omnipotent.' He held Nick's gaze. 'Tell me what happened.'

Nick babbled out the whole story again. Katie listened much more intently this time, actually taking in his words instead of looking for ways to refute them. It was harder to be sceptical when the evidence was all around you.

Nick tried not to look at the faces of his slow-motion classmates while he was speaking. There was something horribly voyeuristic and invasive about it, even though logically it was no different from what he would have been seeing at normal speed.

Cavanagh nodded along at several points, but his face betrayed little. When Nick was done, he sat back and let out an explosive sigh. 'Wow,' he said, pushing back his hair. 'This is . . . wow. A debt of service . . . I always knew Grey was arrogant, but I've never known him take this kind of risk before. He must be getting more and more confident of his abilities.'

'How is it a risk?' Katie wondered. 'Any way you slice it, Nick is the one getting screwed.'

'Oh, the bargain itself is no risk to him,' Cavanagh agreed. 'Grey never sets up any deal that isn't a win-win. But that *bracelet* . . .' He shook his head in wonder. 'Don't you see, Nick? It identifies you as an employee of the shop. It empowers you to open and seal locks, and touch things that were guarded against everyone but Grey himself before.'

'But what good does that do me?' Nick demanded. 'I want to get *out*, not in!'

Cavanagh leaned forward excitedly. 'Ah, but that's just it. Getting *in* is the secret to getting out!' He grinned in triumph, but reined himself in a little at their expressions of confusion. 'Grey draws his strength from the orbs in his collection,' he explained more calmly. 'With every trade he sets up, he makes a profit and gains a little more power. By this stage, he's effectively invincible in a head-to-head battle – no one else can match the resources he has at his disposal. When he places a magical binding on a customer, there's no way that anybody else can break it.'

'So Grey's the only one who can break one of his bargains?' Katie said grimly.

'Yes. Occasionally – very occasionally – there's some kind of loophole that can be exploited: a way to fulfil the letter of the agreement but not the spirit, or to force Grey into defaulting on his end. But he's not at all stupid, and those kind of opportunities are rare. A lot of the time he traps people into deliberately open-ended deals – like yours.' He flicked his gaze sideways to Nick.

'Then what hope is there?' Nick shook his head.

'More than you'd think.' Cavanagh gave a sharp smile. 'You see, Grey isn't quite the master of magic he'd like to have you believe. He didn't invent the orbs – he stole the secret of them from an order of monks centuries ago. That first orb, the master orb, was never used for anything like this. It was a sacred artefact, an instrument for testing souls. It could see into the hearts of those who made vows before it, and tell genuine men of faith from liars and oathbreakers.'

His face darkened. 'But then Edmund Grey – who at that time was a quite ordinary man, with a small natural talent for magical trickery – encountered the order, and learned about the powers of the master orb. He stole it from them, and perverted its sacred magic to set up his empire, trapping people into magical vows it would kill them to break. He's gathered more power than any one man could possibly need, yet he stays holed up in his shop, addicted to gathering more. By the time the order caught up with him, he was already too powerful to be attacked directly. They knew he had the orb, but they couldn't take it back.'

There was too much passion in his voice for someone just reciting ancient history. Nick's eyes dropped to the crystal pendant resting against Cavanagh's chest. An orb held in cupped hands.

'You're one of them,' he realized.

Cavanagh gave a slow nod. 'One of the very last descendants of the order. I've been waiting all my life for a chance to recover the sacred orb – and now it's here. It's you, Nick. With that bracelet you wear, you can get past all Grey's defences. *You* can get the orb back and set everybody trapped in one of these bargains free.'

'No.' Nick rocked back in his chair, shaking his head. 'I can't steal from Mr Grey!' Just the thought of it was enough to induce a panic attack. 'He'll know! I . . .' He pointed helplessly at the bracelet on his wrist.

'He doesn't know you're meeting me now,' Cavanagh said. 'He doesn't know a lot of things. I can make sure he doesn't even know you're in the shop.'

'He'll be able to work it out afterwards!' It wouldn't be hard for Grey to figure out the thief with only one possible suspect.

'He'll be powerless afterwards!' Cavanagh said

forcefully. 'He might not even live. He took the master orb hundreds of years ago. It can only be the magic he's drawing from the orbs that's allowed him to stay alive this long.'

Nick shook his head, looking down at his hands. 'I don't know . . .' he said miserably.

Steal from Mr Grey? Why not shove his arm into a piranha tank while he was at it? Even if he somehow managed to get away with the orb, Grey would immediately know it had been him. And even if Grey didn't have any magic left, he could still come round to Nick's house and *stab* him. He was hardly going to take the loss of his entire business lying down.

Nick might be better off just taking his chances with the deal that he already had. Surely Grey had to deliver what he'd agreed to *sometime* . . .

'I know it's a scary proposition.' Cavanagh squeezed his arm. 'But a chance like this might never come again. Trust me – Grey has no intention of letting you go free. If you abide by his terms, you'll be a slave for ever. But if you help me, I can release you, and all the other victims, from his clutches. I can stop him ever doing anything like this again.' He drew back and stood, reluctantly closing his hand around the crystal pendant. 'I have to go. I can't hold this illusion much longer. But we'll talk again – and soon. This is our only chance, Nick. We have to take it.'

He backed away out of the classroom. Abruptly, everything sprang back to colourful, chaotic life, and people were suddenly in different positions from where they'd seemed to be before. A whole set of diagrams and explanations had appeared on the board, bags had jumped from desks to the floor or vice versa, there were textbooks on Mrs Naples's desk in the space where Cavanagh had just been sitting. No one else in the class seemed aware that anything unusual had happened.

Nick stared at his watch in disbelief as the bell rang. Had an entire hour of class gone by while they were sealed inside Cavanagh's bubble? He got up and ran to the door, but there was no sign of the man in the corridor outside. 'He's gone,' he said to Katie.

'Or we just can't see him.' She stared at Nick, mouth slightly open. 'Nick . . . did that just happen?'

Nick gave a sour smile and started packing up his stuff. 'Welcome to my world.'

* * *

'You've got to do it,' Katie said as they lined up outside English waiting for break to be over.

'Steal this master orb thing?' Nick laid his head back against the corridor wall and shook it miserably. 'It's impossible. I'd never get away with it.'

'If it's really the only way you're ever going to get free—'

'It's practically suicide! Katie, you saw what this guy Cavanagh can do. Well, Grey is much, *much* more powerful. And I'm supposed to somehow take this thing from right under his nose? I might as well go ahead and kill myself now.'

'Oh, like you're not doing that already?' She glared at him. 'Have you looked in a mirror lately? You look like the living dead!'

'Yeah, well, if Mr Grey catches me stealing from him, I'll be the *dead* dead!' he snapped back. 'This is not a computer game, Katie! I don't get to go back to the start of the level if I mess it up.'

'You don't get to ignore it and hope it goes away, either.' She folded her arms across her stomach unhappily. 'You've got to do *something*, Nick. You can't go on like this.'

Nick was saved from making a response by the arrival of their English teacher. He took his seat near the front of the class, where Katie had no chance to badger him without being overheard. He needed time to think.

But the more he chased Cavanagh's plan around his mind, the more impossible it seemed. How could he hope to go against Grey like that – and survive? He just couldn't do it.

'Don't even start, OK?' he groaned as Katie showed up outside his German classroom at the lunch bell. 'I've already made up my mind. I'm not doing it.'

'Nick, you've got to!' Katie said. 'Seriously, what *choice* do you have? You can't just keep working for Grey. Even if he is planning to let you go someday, you've got no idea when. It could be ten, twenty years from now. It could be when you're *dead*. You have to . . . Nick?'

She turned and veered back to where Nick had stopped dead in the middle of the corridor, his right hand clenched in a fist. 'What is it?' Katie reached out to touch his arm, then yanked her fingers back with a hiss. 'Jesus! You're boiling!'

'Collection,' Nick said tightly. He thrust his hand into his bag and closed it around the latest orb. 'I've got to go.' He turned round, looking for the fastest route out of school.

'No, wait, Nicky—'

'I can't!' He threw up his hands helplessly as he jogged backwards towards the doors. 'I seriously have to go right *now*.' After yesterday, he daren't risk being late. 'I'll talk to you later, I promise.'

Katie swore. 'This is *exactly* what I'm talking about, Nick!' she yelled after him.

He tossed her a wave over his shoulder as he ran.

Nick had only minutes to get to his target, a Hannah Armstrong of Bell Street. The address was mercifully close to school, but he still had to sneak out the back way, praying no one would spot him and demand to see a lunch pass.

Bell Street was a cluster of neat bungalows with pristine gardens and few cars parked on drives at this time of the day. Nick found the right house and loitered in front of it for a moment, resting his foot on the low wall to undo and retie his laces. He could hear piano music drifting out of an open window. It was a muted, melancholy piece, not anything he recognized but beautifully played.

Nick had a sickening feeling he knew what he was here for.

The house had a pretty, well-kept garden full of early-blooming flowers. They'd been picked by someone with an eye for colour, and the overall effect was warm and welcoming. The plate on the door that gave the house number was shaped like a hedgehog.

Reluctantly Nick pressed the bell. It gave a low, melodic chime, and the piano music stopped. A moment later he saw a shadow approaching through the distortion of the textured glass.

The door was opened by a pretty black girl in chunky, red-framed glasses, and the same school uniform he was wearing. He didn't know her, except as a vaguely familiar face, so she had to be in Year Ten or younger.

He *really* hoped she was answering the door for her mother.

'Are you . . . Hannah?' Nick asked, after a beat of hesitation.

'Hi . . .?' she said blankly.

Shit.

'What?' she blurted as the silence hung on. 'Am I in trouble? I've got a lunch pass. I signed out and everything.'

'Er, no, it's nothing to do with that.' He hastily peeled back his sleeves to show her the bracelet. 'I'm Nick Spencer, and I work for a shop called Bargains in the town. I think you have some kind of deal with them . . .?'

The girl's eyes widened in shock and dismay. 'Are you here to take the crystal ball back?'

'Um . . .'

'Because I thought it might have been a mistake – he practically gave it to me, and I didn't even know it would do anything, but you can't take it back because I really, really need it, and—'

Nick was helpless under the stream of nervous babble. He held up his hands. 'Um . . . maybe you should just tell me exactly what happened,' he said, heart sinking. 'Can I come in?'

Hannah led him into a well-furnished living room that was lined with books and dominated by a large piano. Nick didn't know much about instruments, but it was obviously far more expensive than the ones they had at school. She appeared to be alone in the house, and he wondered if that was exactly why the bracelet had sent him here at this particular moment.

He perched awkwardly on the edge of a chair as she spilled out her story with the desperation of someone who'd been dying to meet a person safe to tell it to. The way it started was uncomfortably familiar. Hannah had stumbled across Bargains in the search for a leaving gift for her mum, who was being forced to work out in New Zealand for a year to keep her job.

'Then I found the crystal ball, and it was *perfect*. It was so pretty, and the family inside it looked just like us . . . it was spooky. It was, like, the more I looked at it, the better the resemblance got, you know?'

He knew. Nick nodded grimly.

'So I really wanted to get it, but I thought it was going to be, like, ninety pounds or something. I was even going to go home and ask my dad if he'd pay for it. But the man just asked me if I played the piano. So

I said yes, and he said –' she scrunched her face up in remembrance – ' "Your musical talent is enough to pay for it", or something like that. So I assumed he'd, like, seen me at one of my concerts or something. I couldn't believe he was just giving it to me, but he said I could take it.' She wrung her hands anxiously.

'Yeah.' Nick rubbed the back of his head to ward off a building headache.

'And then I gave it to my mum, and, like, that very second, the phone rang. And her boss said that they'd decided not to move everything out to New Zealand all at once, but they were going to keep some of the staff at the local office, and my mum was one of the people they wanted to stay.' Her delighted, beaming smile faded into something more uneasy. 'It was the crystal ball, wasn't it? I looked inside it after, and the picture was completely gone. It was like a magic spell.'

'Yeah,' Nick agreed, with a grimace. 'Yeah, it was.'

She shook her head tearfully. 'You can't take it back. *Please.* I'll pay for it somehow, I promise. I don't want her to have to go.'

Nick swallowed; Hannah's obvious distress was

unpleasantly contagious. 'I'm not here to take it back,' he said. 'The shopkeeper thinks you already agreed a payment. You, er . . .' He stopped and cleared his throat. 'He thinks you said that he could take your musical talent.'

The shopkeeper must make deals like this all the time. Not everyone would be carrying around a convenient symbol of their talent like Nick's sketches. No wonder Grey's customers were reluctant to pay up – they had no idea they'd agreed to pay anything at all.

Hannah stared at him, eyes confused and still glassy with tears. 'You mean . . . so I wouldn't be good at the piano any more?'

'No.' He looked down at his fingers. 'You, er . . . you wouldn't be able to play at all.'

She was silent for a long moment. He couldn't look at her.

'But . . . my mum would stay?' she said finally.

'Yeah . . . You don't have to take the deal,' Nick blurted out abruptly, though he had no authority to say so. 'I mean, if you didn't know what you were agreeing to . . .'

'But if I don't, my mum's still going to leave.'

'Yeah, but—'

'I'll take the deal,' Hannah said. Her face was pinched with distress, but utterly resolute. 'You can take my piano playing. I just want Mum to stay.'

Nick shook his head miserably. 'You don't know what it's going to be like,' he said. 'You'll lose everything you ever learned. For ever. It's not—'

'I don't care.' She stood up. 'It's my decision.' Her determination cracked for just a second, and she gestured at the piano. 'Am I, um . . . am I allowed to finish the piece I was playing first?'

'Yeah, sure,' Nick said thickly. 'Of course you can.'

He stared down at the carpet as she settled herself on the piano stool and began to play.

He'd never liked classical music much. He didn't hate it; it just didn't do anything for him. At least the 1960s stuff his mum liked to blast when she was doing housework was kind of catchy, even if it was totally dated. But with classical music it always seemed like the rhythm was off, the combination of sounds subtly wrong. He could listen to it, but somehow he didn't quite get it.

He got it now.

The piano piece was like nothing he would have called good music, but it had a mournful tone to it that made him close his eyes. It dragged up the sense of loss that had dogged him ever since that fateful art lesson, making him feel choked up and small. His stomach ached and goosepimples rose up on his cheeks and arms. When it was over, he swallowed hard and kept his eyes on the pattern of the carpet until he heard Hannah stand up.

'So,' she said, with more emotional control than he had. 'What happens now?'

'You, er, you give me that piece of music you were playing from, and then we shake hands.'

Nick was praying that Hannah would change her mind, but she passed the sheet music to him and held her hand out with solemn dignity. As they shook, the bracelet tightened and energy pulsed through him, and it took all his self-control not to crush her fingers. The outlines of the room warped and wavered, and then grew still.

'Is that it?' she asked, her eyes deep pools of welling tears.

'Yeah, um . . . that's it.' He had to clear his throat again.

'But I don't *feel* any different,' she said, studying the palms of her hands as if they held the answers.

'You will,' he said, from bitter personal experience.

Hannah looked up at him. 'I don't care,' she said, though her lower lip trembled a little. 'My mum's going to stay now. And that's what matters.'

And Nick had nothing to say to that at all. Maybe she was right. Maybe she wasn't. But however much she might have felt this was the only choice she could make, Nick knew exactly how much she was going to regret it.

He let himself out. When the door had closed behind him, he rested his head back against it for a moment, and just breathed.

As he started up the pathway, he heard a single, plaintive note repeated over and over on the piano.

Nick brushed back angry tears as he started back along Bell Street. He felt like the lowest kind of thief, stealing priceless treasures from children. Mr Grey had just forced him into committing the same crime that had ruined his own life. What was worse was that he'd blackmailed Hannah into it with the threat of her mother leaving if she didn't play along. The fact that it was Mr Grey's threat, not his own, didn't make him feel any better.

Part of him wanted to just throw the orb against the nearest wall and watch it shatter. Why should the shop get it? Grey had no right to take these things from people. But Nick was afraid that if he did, Hannah's talent would be lost for ever. At least while it was in the orb, she still had a slim chance of getting it back.

He thought again of Cavanagh's offer. *Was* it the only way out? It seemed more like a noose to strangle himself with than a lifeline. He wanted to *escape* Mr Grey's potential wrath, not bring it down on his head. And unlike Cavanagh, Nick didn't have handy magic powers to hide himself if Grey came after him, wanting revenge.

But he wasn't sure how long he could keep on working for Bargains, either. The collections were killing him, and he had no idea if any end was in sight. Nick was starting to feel like the grim reaper, stalking around the town leaving shattered lives in his wake. What would he have to take from the next person? A career? A relationship? A body part?

Grey had sold him a thunderstorm in a glass ball. What was that? Some farmer's allotment of rain for his crops? If the shopkeeper could control the *weather* people experienced, what limit was there on his power? Nick could be made to take *anything* from these people. Literally.

He trudged through town towards Bargains, his whole body tense with misery. There was just no way out. Every option he had was impossible. He was utterly, utterly trapped.

As Nick let himself into the shop, his stomach twisted up with nerves. He was sure his meeting with Cavanagh was written all over his face. It seemed impossible that Grey could *not* know they'd been plotting against him. Maybe he would strike Nick down right now instead of waiting for him to try something.

The orb room was deserted. Nick was freshly conscious of the weight of its contents, the lost dreams captured inside each of the glass balls. Behind every one was a customer as miserable and trapped as he was. How had the story ended for them? *Had* it ended, or were they all still slaves to the shopkeeper, as he was? Did they return to Bargains again and again, trying to buy back their treasures and only selling more of themselves in the attempt?

Nick shuddered and quickly moved on. He reached

the door of the office but hesitated, looking towards the stairs. Where did they lead? Was that where Mr Grey kept the master orb?

Nick listened hard, but couldn't hear the faintest hint of movement from below. Maybe Grey wasn't around. He could have gone out to make a collection of his own. Surely even he had to eat and sleep sometimes.

Nick descended the first few steps, painfully aware of his footsteps echoing in the stillness. *This is stupid, this is stupid, this is stupid,* a voice chanted in the back of his head. But maybe he could just take a look, scout around and see if the master orb was down there. See if the theft would actually be possible. He didn't have to do anything irreversible.

There was a door at the foot of the stairs. It was dark, solid wood, engraved with a detailed pattern that matched the one wrapped around his wrist. Nick took a deep breath and laid the palm of his hand directly over the carved eye. He felt something flow from the bracelet down through his palm. When he drew back his hand, the wooden eye had changed from open to shut. He pushed, and the door gave way before him.

Nick stepped through into a vast underground chamber. It was lit by an overhead glow, like firelight, but he couldn't see any place it might be coming from. The floor and walls were worn-down stone, far older than the brickwork upstairs, and the ceiling was low. The room looked huge, far bigger than the school assembly hall, but it was impossible to see how far back it went, as it was filled with a maze of dark-wood shelves like those in the orb room.

But these shelves weren't lined with orbs. Instead, they were crammed with every kind of object imaginable. In places they seemed to be organized by content, while in others they looked absolutely random. Nick saw papers and photographs everywhere; books, shoes, toys, jewellery, musical instruments, tools . . .

With a sudden, deathly chill, he understood what he was looking at. Tokens – like Hannah's sheet music that he had in his bag right now, like the trophy he'd taken from Mullen. Like whatever it was Tariq had given away when he first signed up to sell his own flesh piece by piece. Every one of these items represented a deal. A person. Someone who had sold a part of their life and soul to Mr Grey.

There must have been a hundred thousand things on the shelves. More. The orbs in the room upstairs were only a tiny, tiny tip of the whole iceberg. This collection – no, it was too big to be a collection; this *warehouse*, this *museum* – told the real story. Every one of these items was a stolen dream.

How many people had Grey enslaved over the years?

Nick's eyes slid to a vast stack of papers. Was his sketch in there somewhere? Or was it buried elsewhere in another similar pile? Did Grey need to keep these things to enforce his bargains, or did he just enjoy walking among them, basking in the evidence of all the people he'd cheated over the years?

Nick's jaw tightened. Where the hell was that master orb? If he found it, he was taking it now. This couldn't be allowed to continue.

He took a step forward – and *felt*, rather than heard, the slither of movement behind him.

'Mr Spencer,' the shopkeeper said, so close that his breath stirred the hairs on the back of Nick's neck. 'Is there any particular reason you are sneaking around places you do not have permission to be?'

Nick closed his eyes and tried to suppress a whimper. 'I was . . . I was looking for you, sir,' he finally managed to say, pressing his teeth together in a wince.

'Perhaps,' Mr Grey said, in a tone of flat disbelief. 'After all, why should it occur to you to retrieve your next collection from the same place it has been every *other* time?'

'I—'

'Take the orb *from the desk*,' Grey enunciated very clearly. 'Leave the other one in its place. And *never* come down here again.'

'Yes, sir,' he squeaked, and he fled back up the stairs.

Nick was too rattled to go back to school. Instead he hid in the toilets in the Westfield Centre until he felt less like he was going to puke, and then went to the park. He sat on a bench in the freezing cold, looking at nothing and trying to think about nothing. If anyone spotted him as a truant, they didn't bother to report him.

He had no idea what he was going to do. The right choice was obvious – and impossible. Someone else was going to have to be Cavanagh's hero. Nick didn't have the guts for it. He still didn't know where the master orb was, and he wasn't about to defy Grey by going down to the basement level again. He'd almost wet himself this time – and he didn't have to be told that he would be given no second chances. If he went back again, he was dead.

The underground warehouse was evidence that the shop had seen thousands upon thousands of victims over the years. Why was Nick the one who was supposed to do something about it? Was he the only one who'd been stupid enough to return and beg for a way to earn back what he'd paid? He hadn't known what he was doing! He banged the bracelet against the edge of the bench in frustration.

Katie sent him a text at the end of school; he replied with a terse, I'M OK, and turned off his phone. He wasn't in the mood for company.

Procrastinating over going home, Nick found himself thinking of Tariq. Bracelet or no bracelet, he was stuck in the same situation, a perpetual slave to the shop. Right now, Nick could do with commiserating with someone who actually understood what Mr Grey was like and why it was so impossible to stand up to him.

He hiked all the way over to Goldbrook Avenue, only to find that Tariq wasn't in. He swore a few times, and thumped his head against the wall. Apparently, the entire universe was conspiring against him. He scrawled a brief, and probably incoherent, note about Cavanagh, shoved it under the door, and turned round to limp back to his mum's house.

Greg was the only one in the house when Nick arrived. 'Where's Rachel?' Nick asked, as he slipped off his coat.

'I haven't seen her.' Greg shrugged unconcernedly, eyes fixed on the computer screen as he blasted zombies.

'Well, didn't Mrs Morgan drop her off?' Nick tugged his tie off and threw it on the bed.

Greg shrugged again. 'I don't know. Oh wow, did you see that? His head just *exploded*!' He tapped keys gleefully.

Nick checked his watch. Rachel went home with

her friend Sarah after school, but Sarah's mum should have brought her back by now. The only usual break in the routine was . . .

. . . Thursdays.

Nick swore and jumped up. 'I was supposed to pick her up from dancing!'

Greg burst into laughter. 'Oh, you *dick*.'

'Shut up! It's not *funny*.' He frantically raced to put his coat and shoes back on. Rachel's dancing class finished at half past four, which meant she was probably sitting waiting for him already. His mother was going to kill him.

Greg hadn't got over the hilarity quite yet. 'You *forgot* Rachel. You are such an idiot.'

'Shut *up*, Greg!' He raced back down the stairs and slammed out into the street. Guilt made his stomach do backflips. He'd be lucky if he got down to the community centre before five. Rachel was going to be hopping mad. He just hoped she had the sense to actually stay put. She had a bad tendency to believe she was more grown up than she really was.

Nick tried her phone, but it was switched off, and probably still in her bedroom. Mum had banned her from taking it to school after one telling-off too many. He swore again, realizing that he should have stopped to look up the number for her dance teacher. Oh, Jesus! He did not *need* this kind of extra responsibility right now.

What made it worse was that he couldn't even blame Mr Grey directly. He hadn't been out on a job, he'd just flat-out forgotten his half-sister. Right now he couldn't keep track of what day it was, never mind where he was supposed to be.

To his relief, Rachel and her teacher were both still there when he arrived, although the hall was otherwise empty. 'Ah, Nick, there you are.' Her teacher gave him a bright smile. 'We were beginning to get worried.'

'*I* wasn't worried,' Rachel said sullenly. Nick knew he was the one in the wrong, but he still wanted to smack her for the attitude.

'I'm sorry. I forgot it was Thursday.' He forced a patient tone.

She screwed her face up in disgust. 'I've been sitting here for *ages*. How can you forget what *day* it is?'

Her whining was going right through his head.

And for somebody who was complaining about having to wait, she didn't seem to be in much of a hurry to get moving. Nick let out a sharp huff of breath. 'Look, some of us have bigger things to worry about than boy bands, OK?' he snapped. 'Now, can you *get a move on*?'

'You're such a *jerk*,' Rachel said, and – he was sure – deliberately moved even slower.

Their mother opened the door for them as they were coming up the path. 'Oh, good, you're back. Everything all right?'

'*No*,' Rachel said, with a venomous scowl. 'He didn't come to get me!'

Nick sighed and scrubbed his hands over his face. 'Sorry, Mum,' he said. 'I just completely forgot.' He leaned back against the wall, feeling utterly exhausted.

'Happens to all of us in our old age,' she teased. But she paused in the doorway, studying him more closely. 'You all right, sugar? You look a bit pale.'

'Yeah, fine,' he said, forcing himself to straighten up and smile. 'Just a bit stressed out at the moment.'

His mum smiled and squeezed his shoulder. 'Don't

worry so much, sweetheart. I know you've got a lot on your plate with the exams coming up, but you just wait – in a couple of months you'll be wondering what all the fuss was about. Try and relax a bit, hmm?'

It was just as well she turned away, because there really wasn't anything he could have trusted himself to say to that.

Nick picked at dinner, unable to muster much appetite even though he'd missed lunch. Rachel was still sulking, and Greg seemed to be twice as annoying as usual – although that might just have been Nick's mood.

He found himself drifting about restlessly. He was too agitated to sit still, yet too worn out to think about doing anything. TV gave him a headache, and he couldn't concentrate to read. He kept reaching for his sketchbook and trying to force something out onto the page, as stupid and pointless an activity as poking a wobbly tooth with his tongue. The results never changed, and it only made him steadily more frustrated.

At eight o'clock he gave up and took a shower, intending to go bed early. There was no way he would sleep, but it wasn't as if his being up was getting anything accomplished.

Nick stood under the pounding water for a long time, wondering if he was ever going to be able to relax again. He felt like he could sleep for a year and still not catch up on the energy he'd lost. In fact, that idea was quite tempting – to just go to sleep and wake up in a few months, when all of this was *over*. Let somebody else solve it for him in the meantime.

He stayed in the shower until his muscles protested at standing so long and his skin was sore from the relentless spray.

It was only when he finally stepped out that he realized it wasn't the shower irritating his skin at all.

The bracelet was heating up again.

'What? *No!*' Nick stared at his arm in disbelief. 'I've done this once today already!'

Two collections in one day? He was stretched to his limits just coping with one. The thought of going back out again so soon turned his stomach.

And what if it didn't end there? Would he get back home after this job and immediately be called out on another one? Would he even be allowed to sleep, or would Grey just run him ragged until he died of exhaustion?

This had to stop.

The bracelet, indifferent to his feelings, continued to get hotter. Without the shower as a distraction, it was rapidly climbing up the scale towards unbearable. There was no possibility of ignoring it. And the orb was back in his room.

Abandoning the pyjamas he'd brought to change into, Nick wrapped a towel around his waist and sprinted for the bedroom.

Greg, still at the computer, yelled in protest. 'Argh! Jesus! I don't want to look at you naked! Trauma! Childhood trauma!' He cringed and shielded his eyes.

'Shut up, Greg.' Nick stuffed his hand into his school bag before the glow from the orb could spill out and fill the whole room. He took two seconds to sigh in blessed relief at the cessation of pain, then grabbed fresh clothes from the chest of drawers to pull on.

'Where are you going then?' Greg demanded as Nick laced up his shoes.

'Round to my dad's.' It was getting easier to lie. He couldn't remember the last time he'd said something to his family that was more than half true.

He left the wet towel on the bed, grabbed his bag and jogged downstairs.

His mum and James looked up as he poked his head into the living room. 'Where are you off to in such a hurry?' his mum asked, putting down her book.

Nick grimaced. 'There's something else I've forgotten.' He had no trouble sounding like he wanted to scream with frustration. 'Coursework. Round at Dad's, on the computer. It's due in tomorrow – I've got to go and finish it.'

'Oh, *Nick*!' his mother groaned.

'Want me to drive you over there?' James offered, getting to his feet.

Nick shook his head quickly. 'No, um, I'll just walk, it's easier. Er, I don't know if I'll be coming back or not. Depends how late it gets. I might stay there.' Maybe if he sold his father the same story after the collection, his parents wouldn't compare notes on when he left versus when he arrived.

'Nick—' His mother was clearly about to protest, but he didn't wait around to hear it.

'Yeah. I've really got to get this done. I'll see you

tomorrow probably. Bye!' Nick called from the hall. He ran out of the front door before there was time for a response.

It was raining outside, the streets dark and damp. He sprinted all the way to the main road, trying to get away before his mum or stepdad could catch up with him and offer him a lift. He really couldn't afford to get trapped into actually going to his dad's.

Not that Nick knew where he was going. He stopped in a bus shelter to pull the orb out of his bag. *Henry Jenkins, 68 Charleston Road.* He had twenty-two minutes to get there.

Fortunately Nick knew the address – one of the old streets down the hill from the university. He made his way towards it, pulling the collar of his coat up around his chin.

The benefits of his warm shower were gone in a matter of minutes. The earlier drizzle had evolved into the kind of icy rain that hit hard as pellets and drove into him almost horizontally. He had to keep his head bowed low to avoid being stung in the face as it plastered his hair to his scalp and his jeans to his legs. The orange-gold glow of the streetlights made the puddled streets dazzlingly bright.

It was a long, long walk to Charleston Road. Nick was the only pedestrian crazy enough to be out in the storm. He trudged along the streets in grim resignation, not bothering to try and race to avoid the weather.

Charleston Road was full of little grey houses with tiny strips of garden and low-set basement windows. Rumbling bass music poured out of several of the residences, and a lot of the haphazardly parked cars were older than he was. This was the student and low-income part of town. The narrow, sunken pavement was uneven, and it was hard not to stagger down it faster than he meant to.

His target, number sixty-eight, had little to distinguish it from its neighbours. The door he stopped outside was battered, and discoloured net curtains hung in the windows. The lights were on behind them, but Nick had to press the doorbell three times before he got any response. He used the extra time to shake some of the water from his coat and hair. The rain had slackened from a downpour to a steady patter now, but it was too late for Nick to look anything other than drowned; the man who opened the door to him clearly thought so.

He was grey-haired and balding, in his late fifties at least, and his face was pinched in a curious frown. He wore a baggy knitted jumper and greenish-brown trousers that looked like he'd picked them out decades ago, and rarely washed them since. Nick found it hard not to cringe away from him.

'Henry Jenkins?' he said unenthusiastically.

The man gave him a toothy smile that wasn't so much charming as creepy. 'That's right,' he said jovially. 'What brings you to my door, young man? Just out for a swim in the neighbourhood?' He tittered at his own weak joke.

Nick didn't bother replying with a false smile. He pushed back layers of sodden sleeves to display the shop bracelet. 'I'm here to make a collection for Bargains,' he said.

'Of course, of course!' Jenkins's eyebrows shot up and his body language immediately turned sycophantic. 'Come in! Welcome to my humble abode.' He gave a nervous chuckle.

Nick entered reluctantly. The house was not as disgusting as he'd feared, although it had a stale smell. The rooms were small and dingy, cluttered with furniture and ornaments that wouldn't have looked out of place in a downmarket second-hand shop. Mr Jenkins, it seemed, was the kind of man who never threw anything away.

He led Nick into the living room, where there was an old TV perched on a coffee table and a set of mismatched armchairs that had been repaired with insulating tape.

'Would you like to sit down? Oh, no, I suppose you're a bit wet.' Jenkins rubbed his hands together nervously. 'Can I get you something to drink? Tea, coffee . . .'

Nick had no desire to linger in this creepy man's house any longer than he had to. 'Um, no thank you. I'm, er . . . I can't really stay very long.'

Jenkins nodded understandingly. 'Of course. You must be very busy. I didn't realize Mr Grey had taken on a new apprentice.'

Nick was sure his dismay at that must be written all over his face. 'Oh, no, I'm not – it's a temporary position,' he said hastily.

'Ah. I see.' Nick couldn't help but notice that Jenkins's fawning attitude cooled markedly at that news.

Nick cleared his throat and straightened up. 'You're aware of the terms of the deal?' he said, in as good an impression of Mr Grey's imperious tone as he could. It was pure spite, but oddly enough Jenkins didn't seem to take it that way. In fact, his eyes positively lit up.

'Yes, of course. More than reasonable, so far as I'm concerned,' he said smugly.

Nick blinked. 'It is?' he said doubtfully. Surely Grey's prices were *never* reasonable.

But Jenkins seemed only too happy to brag about the terms of his deal. 'Five years of my life for un-limited wealth? I could still live another fifty years – every one of them in luxury!'

'You signed away five years of your *life*?' Nick couldn't keep the appalled look off his face.

Mr Jenkins scowled at him. 'Of course you wouldn't understand. You're a child. You have no idea what it's like to be overlooked for decades, to be constantly passed over for reward while the less deserving climb the ladder. Life isn't fair, boy. Those of us with genuine abilities are kept down by the ones who have the right connections, by mediocre people who won't threaten the status quo. In a just world I'd be earning a six-figure salary by now. I'm just taking back what I deserve.'

'Right,' Nick said flatly. Who was he to argue if this idiot wanted to trade away years of his life for such a selfish reward? This was one collection that wasn't going to keep him awake at night. He pulled the orb out of his school bag and held it in his left hand. 'Then it's agreed.' He held out his right for the man to shake.

'It's agreed,' Jenkins echoed. 'And you can tell your Mr Grey that if it doesn't work, I expect—' His words cut off as their hands connected and energy surged through both of them.

But something wasn't right.

Instead of the bracelet's usual pulse, Nick felt a terrific *pull*, like the suction of a hungry whirlpool. The room flashed from warm to icy cold in a heartbeat, and the clouds of breath that puffed out of Jenkins's mouth spiralled towards the band on Nick's wrist. The light from the bulb in the ceiling refracted as if even the light rays were being pulled off course. Nick had to close his eyes against the pressure as his skin rippled and stretched.

Jenkins's fingers had gone cold and slack in his own, but he couldn't let go of them, couldn't force his muscles to unlock. Nick's whole body trembled and juddered, and he could feel all his joints beginning to pull out of alignment, his flesh stretched to the point of tearing.

Then, as suddenly as it had started, the pull was gone, and the force of its ending smashed into him like a tidal wave. A firework display of multicoloured lights went off behind his eyes and shattered into sparks.

As the lights faded out, so did he.

Nick woke to a faceful of scratchy carpet. He felt utterly wrecked, as if he'd run a complete marathon and just this second collapsed at the finish line. Every single part of his body ached and burned.

He opened his eyes. Even his eyelids were sore. It took a moment to pull his worm's-eye view of the world into focus. He found he was staring at the foot of an armchair.

'Ow,' he said, rather inadequately. He checked over his battered body, and realized he was still gripping Mr Jenkins's slack hand. His 'client' must have been knocked unconscious too.

What the hell had just happened? Had he done something wrong? For a moment Nick felt a stab of hope. Was the bracelet bust? But no, he could still feel it there around his wrist. Even if something had gone wrong, he hadn't escaped from it.

He pushed himself up on one arm. 'Mr Jenkins? I think—' The rest of the words froze solid in his mouth as he got his first good look at the man lying beside him.

He was holding the hand of a corpse.

Nick let go and jerked back in a pure reflex action, almost knocking the chair behind him off its feet. He scrambled up into it and drew his legs in, staring down at Jenkins in mesmerized revulsion.

He'd never seen a dead body before, but there was no mistaking Jenkins's state for unconsciousness. The man's skin was an ugly, waxy grey-white and his face had swollen hugely. His cheek had taken on a purplish hue where it pressed against the carpet, as if all his blood had drained downwards now that no heartbeat kept it pumping. His blue eyes were still open, but they were unfocused, blank and cloudy.

And he was utterly, horribly still. Far more still than any human being could be on purpose. Nick had never realized how *visible* it was that someone was breathing until he saw someone who wasn't.

He wrenched his gaze away as soon as he could, but he knew it was an image that would never leave him.

Nick couldn't stay in the room two seconds longer. He stood on the chair and stepped from it to the next one, keeping the maximum distance between him and Jenkins's corpse. He jumped down and crashed through the door into the hall.

He would have run right out to the street and kept running, if a more pressing need hadn't beckoned. Nick yanked open a door that he was relieved to find led to the bathroom, and promptly threw up in the sink.

He hung over the basin miserably until the fact that the door was still open sank in. In a burst of paranoia he spun round to slam it shut and pulled the bolt across. Then he sat down with his back against it and tried very hard not to cry.

It was a long time before any sort of conscious thought came back.

The first thought that really penetrated was that he was freezing. He was sitting on a tiled floor wearing wet clothes, and he'd been there so long he was shivering. Nick stood up, his muscles still quaking, and pressed his palms flat against the radiator until they hurt.

It was only as he drew them away that he thought, *Fingerprints*.

His prints would be all over the house. His *DNA* would be all over the house. It would be on Jenkins. He'd seen enough forensic shows to know you couldn't scrub that kind of thing off. You couldn't make a perfectly clean crime scene.

Was this a crime scene? Was he a murderer? He'd shaken hands with Jenkins, and then . . .

This was all wrong. This hadn't been the deal. Jenkins had agreed to give up five years of his life – not *all* of it. He hadn't—

'Shit,' Nick said out loud, in horrified dismay. He stared at himself in the mirror.

Jenkins had given up five years of his life. But what if he hadn't *had* five years to give? What if he'd been going to die of a heart attack, or liver failure, or who knew what before that time was up? And then when he'd sealed the deal, his body had aged through five years in the space of a second, and . . .

'Shit,' Nick said again. His legs suddenly felt like rubber, and he sat down hard on the floor.

Jenkins might have been an unpleasant, selfish little man, but he hadn't known what he was agreeing to any more than Nick had. He'd thought he was getting a great deal.

Had Mr Grey known? Nick wanted to believe that he hadn't, that not even he could have guessed Jenkins would die before the years he'd traded were up. But in truth he knew it made no difference. Grey would have accepted the deal whether he'd known the result or not. He didn't care if his customers got what they wanted – only that they paid the price.

And Nick was the one collecting the payments. He hadn't signed the death warrant, but he'd been the executioner.

He got to his feet and threw up again. He didn't have much food left to lose, but he kept spitting into the sink anyway. He swilled water around his mouth again and again. There was a dead man less than a dozen paces away, and he wouldn't be dead if Nick hadn't shaken his hand.

He couldn't stop shivering. What the hell was he going to do now?

He didn't want to stay in the same house as . . . the body, but he didn't feel like he had a right to leave. Shouldn't he at least call somebody? The police, or an ambulance, or something? But what could he possibly say? He couldn't explain why he was here, how Jenkins had died, who was responsible for the killing . . . Just reporting the death would turn it into a murder investigation.

It *was* a murder. But not one where the man responsible could possibly be caught. If it was recognized as anything other than a natural death, the only one in the frame for it was Nick.

He let out a bitter snort that was close to a sob.

Mr Grey couldn't have stitched him up more neatly if he'd planned it. Perhaps he had. Nick could either fail to report the death – which, he was pretty sure, made him an accessory or something – or he could do the right thing and end up charged with murder. And what if someone had seen him entering the house?

He might end up in police custody anyway. And then what would he do if they wanted him to take the bracelet off, or it started heating up while he was locked in a cell?

Nick stared down at the metal band. Such a simple, delicate-looking thing . . . And yet it was an inescapable prison. As long as he wore it, he was forced to be whatever Mr Grey wanted him to be.

Even a murderer.

He sniffed, and wiped his eyes with the heels of his hands.

Cavanagh. He had to accept Cavanagh's help. As crazy as his plan had seemed when he first proposed it, it was the only way Nick was ever going to get out of this. He knew now that it was worth *any* price to escape. If only he'd agreed to steal the master orb this morning before any of this had happened . . .

He cut off that line of thought before it led to a panic attack. Now all he could think about was the corpse in the front room. What the hell was he going to *do*?

He needed help. He wanted to call Cavanagh, but he didn't have the number with him, and anyway there was no way of knowing how long it might take him to arrive. Nick couldn't stand the thought of sitting here for hours, waiting for a rescue that might never even show up.

But there *was* someone else he could call. The only other person who knew about this insane mess. Nick fumbled out his phone and scrolled through the numbers until he got to Katie's.

She answered the phone with obvious annoyance. '*God*, Nick. How long does it take to return a sodding phone call? I've been leaving you messages all day.'

Just the sound of a friendly voice made him burst into tears. He choked out what had happened in a disjointed, garbled fashion.

'Right,' Katie said when he'd finished. He'd never been more grateful for her habit of trying to take charge in a crisis; she sounded tense, but not nearly as freaked out as he was. 'You need to try and stay calm,' she told him.

Nick let out an incredulous snort of almost-laughter. 'Oh, *sure*. Yeah. I'm doing that.' He had a crazy urge to bang the back of his head against the tiled walls until it all just went away.

'Are you *absolutely sure* the guy is dead?' she asked.

A wave of nausea rose up in his throat. 'Yes. Very, very, very sure.' The image of Jenkins lying there rose up every time he closed his eyes. Living people didn't look like that. Ever.

He tried to picture Katie instead, sitting there biting her lip the way she did when she was working out a logic problem in maths. 'Then there's nothing you can do to help him,' she said. 'So forget about Jenkins. You need to get yourself out of the house.'

'But . . .' A million sources of panic fought in his brain. 'Fingerprints!' he blurted desperately. 'My fingerprints are everywhere, they'll—'

'They won't do anything,' she said firmly. 'Nick, you're not a criminal. Nobody has your fingerprints on file. Even if they get them from Jenkins's house, even if they treat this as a murder – which they *won't*, because from what you said, he basically just stopped being alive – they won't have any reason to connect you to the crime. So far as anyone's concerned, you could just be the pizza boy. You practically *are* the pizza boy. You just make deliveries and collect payments. You're not responsible for what this Jenkins bloke ordered, or if it hurt him.'

Nick made a vague noise, knowing she'd only hound him into agreeing if he didn't. The truth was he didn't know quite what to think of his role in these events, and he was trying not to think about it at all.

'Good. Now, where are you?'

'I'm in the bathroom,' he said, wiping his nose with the back of his hand. He was leaning against the wall beside the radiator. He had no idea how long he'd been there, but he didn't feel any warmer.

'Right. Do you have everything you took with you?'

'What?' he said blankly.

'The orb. You must have had an orb, right? Where is it?'

He looked around. It wasn't in the bathroom, and neither was his school bag. He had no memory of putting either of them down. 'Don't know,' he said feebly. 'I think I must have, um . . . I guess I left it in the living room. And my – my school bag.'

'OK. Stay on the phone and go and get them,' Katie directed.

'I can't.' That was where the body was. He couldn't go back in there.

'You have to,' Katie said, kindly but firmly. 'I'll talk you through it. Come on. Just get out of the bathroom first.'

Even that proved to be a chore. Nick's fingers were shaking so badly he had trouble gripping the bolt to pull it back. 'Seriously, Katie, I can't go back in there,' he said into the phone.

'Well, you're going to have to, mate, because no one else is there to do it for you,' she said flatly. 'Come on. One foot in front of the other. Don't think about it – keep moving.'

That was easy for her to say, safe in her own bedroom where there were no dead bodies. Nick only got as far as the living-room door before he froze again. From out here he could just see the soles of Jenkins's feet. If he stayed where he was, he could pretend it was simply a pair of shoes abandoned on the carpet.

'Nick?' Katie prompted after a moment.

'Yeah,' he said thickly. 'Yeah, I'm going.' His heart-beat felt light and fast, like a hummingbird's wings.

He nudged the door further open with his foot. He

didn't look down at Jenkins's body. He couldn't. He deliberately crossed his eyes to render anything he did see out of focus and indistinguishable.

His bag was lying beside an armchair. It was easy enough to shuffle sideways and retrieve it. The orb was a fuzzy crystal blur on the carpet, centimetres away from another pale blur that he wasn't looking at, wasn't looking at, *wasn't looking at* . . .

Nick stretched out so he could hook the orb closer from the greatest distance possible. He rolled it towards him until he could close his fingers around it, then snatched it up and fled the room.

He wasn't sure how long he spent panting for breath in the hall before he remembered the phone in his hand. He lifted it back to his ear. 'Katie?'

'Jesus. Scare the crap out of me, why don't you?' she hissed, sounding truly rattled for the first time. 'Don't just go silent like that. Did you get it?'

'Yeah.' He turned the orb between his fingers, but avoided looking at it. He really, *really* didn't want to know what he might see inside. 'Yeah, and my bag.'

'Good.' Katie let out a ragged sigh, as if she too had been holding her breath. 'OK. Now you can leave. But I think you should come over to my house.'

'It's late – I don't want to wake everybody up,' Nick protested, although weakly. He couldn't face returning to either of his homes. How was he supposed to lie to cover *this*?

'Yeah, well, my mum goes to bed before me half the time anyway. I'll tell her I'm going out to the garage to get some music practice in. Come round to the garage door and I'll let you in. And then we'll call Cavanagh – tonight – and figure out a way to get you free. OK?'

'OK.' Nick swallowed.

'All you've got to do is get yourself to my house. All right? I'll see you in a minute, Nicky.'

When the call was disconnected, it felt like a knife had sliced through his only lifeline.

Somehow, Nick made it to Katie's. He couldn't have said how he'd got there. The journey was a total blank in his mind. He wasn't aware of even *thinking*. He just left Mr Jenkins's house and then it was . . . later, like a film that faded to black and resumed in a different time and place. He didn't know if anyone had seen him leaving.

He was wet, but from persistent drizzle rather than real rain; he was freezing, and his nose was stuffed up, though he didn't know if it was from the weather or from crying. He felt curiously distanced, like he was walking through the half-real world of a hazy dream.

Katie was waiting for him just outside the garage door. The inside was blessedly warm; she and her band used it for their practices, and it was carpeted and furnished with mismatched items that had been exiled from the house over the years. She dragged him over to sit on a beanbag in front of the heater and made him drink a mug of tea with so much sugar it almost made him sick.

'OK?' she asked when he finally met her eyes, pretty much by accident.

'No.' Nick sighed and rested his head back against the wall. His eyes felt hot and sore, as if he had the flu.

Katie patted his shoulder. 'You're doing fine.'

It was a ridiculous thing to say, but somehow it made him feel a little better anyway.

'I called Cavanagh,' she said a moment later. 'Got hung up on like before. Guess we'll have to wait and see if he comes tonight.'

Nick made a noncommittal noise. He had a watch on his left wrist, but it was beyond him to figure out the sequence of mental instructions required to lift it up and look at it.

The time hardly mattered anyway. He couldn't

think about going home right now. He couldn't think about anything. In his head, he was still back in that dingy little room on Charleston Road, seeing the same horrific scene again and again.

How long would it take for someone to find the body? Would anybody even know to look for it? What if Jenkins wasn't missed? Would he just stay there, slumped on his living-room carpet, until one of the neighbours called to complain about the smell . . .?

A sudden surge of bile caught him by surprise, and he swallowed and coughed to stop himself from vomiting. He gripped the brickwork; it felt like the garage was swaying around him.

'Hey. You OK?' Katie asked. He gave her a flash of a weak smile.

Suddenly they heard footsteps echoing on the path outside. The steps paused for a moment, then turned towards the garage. A short, sharp knock rattled the door and Nick exchanged a fearful glance with Katie before she went to open it. He was sure, irrationally *sure*, that it would be a police officer here to arrest him . . .

But as the shutter rolled up, he recognized the thin

figure of Cavanagh. He wore a long black trench coat and his dark hair was now tied back in a ponytail.

He gave them a stern nod. 'Well?' he said. 'Have you made your decision? Will you help me retrieve the master orb?'

And Nick found he could talk again, though the words scraped his throat like a mouthful of glass. 'Yeah,' he said roughly. 'Yeah. I'll do it.'

They would do it, as it turned out. Katie refused to be left behind, and Nick didn't have the heart or energy to argue with her. Maybe he ought to be noble and insist no one else share the danger, but the truth was he was glad of the company. He wasn't sure he could do this alone.

He wasn't sure he could do it at all, but he had no choice. He couldn't make another collection for Grey. He just couldn't.

The three of them made their way down towards the town centre in tense silence. Nick was still chilled to the bone: he felt like he would never be warm again, but he wasn't sure it was anything to do with his damp clothes.

Cavanagh stopped them just before the traffic lights. 'We're about to enter Grey's territory,' he said. 'He'll be able to sense us coming if we get much closer. You particularly,' he told Nick. 'So from here on, I'll need to hide us magically.'

'And that's enough protection?' Katie said dubiously.

Cavanagh's face was serious. 'I've been operating under his nose for many years now. Believe me, if he'd been able to figure out how I was hiding, I wouldn't still be here.'

Nick swallowed hard. 'All right.' But he couldn't help remembering that Cavanagh hadn't been able to hold the magic together indefinitely. 'How much time will we have?'

Cavanagh closed his hand around the crystal pendant. 'I can guarantee an hour. Beyond that . . . I really don't know.'

Nick thought of the vast underground warehouse and sighed. Either they would find the master orb in that time, or they wouldn't. There would be no second chances – and there were no other options.

He nodded his head jerkily. 'OK. Go on then.'

Cavanagh tightened his grip on the pendant and shut his eyes. He mouthed a sequence of words, and Nick felt energy crackle over him, like static crawling over his skin. Colour and motion faded out of the world around them, like a computer game put on pause. The air took on a thicker, murky quality.

Cavanagh opened his eyes, a new tension showing on his face. 'Quickly now,' he said. 'We can't afford to waste a single second.'

They ran for the entrance to the shop, Nick leading the way. Footsteps that should have echoed loudly in the alley sounded strangely muffled, as if slowed to an ooze.

He almost overshot the entrance to Bargains, and had to backtrack a few steps. There was no tug from the bracelet as there usually was when he arrived.

Maybe Cavanagh's magic meant they truly *were* undetectable to Grey.

Even so, Nick opened the door as softly as possible. No amount of urgency could override his instincts, which were screaming for stealth and silence.

The hallway inside was pitch black. 'Are we outside opening hours?' Katie whispered, she too obviously unable to quite believe Grey couldn't hear them.

'He's still here,' Nick said. He was sure the shop-keeper was always around no matter how abandoned the place might look.

'He won't leave unless he has business to take care of,' Cavanagh confirmed. 'And right now, Nick is handling his business.'

'Yeah, but he has to sleep sometime, right?' Katie said. 'Right?' she pushed again when neither of them answered.

Nick felt his way along the corridor. When he found the turning, he could see the cold glow spilling out of the orb room ahead. It was like starlight, bright enough to show its own presence but not to light up anything else. He crept down the hall and entered the room, all his senses on alert for the first hint that Grey was around.

'Whoa!' Katie said in a hushed voice as they passed between the shelves of orbs.

'There's so many . . .' Cavanagh said in a hoarse voice. 'The amount of power rolling out of this place . . .'

Nick drew the orb he'd brought from Jenkins's

house out of his bag and, fumbling, put it onto one of the racks. The idea of the man's *life* going up on sale made him feel sick, but the thought of keeping hold of it was worse.

Hopefully, if they succeeded in their mission, those stolen years wouldn't be Grey's to buy and sell any more. He was pretty sure it was too late for that to help Mr Jenkins. His death hadn't been part of the deal, only a side effect. Reversing the spell might restore his body to the state of a man five years younger, but the magic wouldn't bring him back to life.

Nick rounded the next row of shelves – and stopped dead, his breath freezing solid in his chest. Mr Grey was waiting there for him, face dark with menacing disapproval.

But he wasn't moving. The air stuttered out of Nick's lungs in a gush as he realized what the silver glow of the orbs had disguised. The shopkeeper was frozen by Cavanagh's spell, just like the others in the science classroom earlier. The man's eyes might *seem* to be locked on Nick, but in truth they weren't seeing him at all.

'Sir?' Nick said cautiously. 'I brought the orb back . . . Sir?'

There was no response. Heart in his mouth, Nick slowly edged around the frozen shopkeeper. He felt like he was trying to walk on a tower of jelly cubes. A part of him was *sure* that Grey's black-hole eyes were following his progress, but he didn't move, didn't even seem to be breathing. So it had to be just paranoia. It had to be.

'Through here,' he called back to the others in a low, shaky voice. If Grey was just faking, handing him the rope to hang himself, then he'd just tied the noose . . . but it was too late to turn back now. 'And be careful. He's here.'

Cavanagh sucked in a sharp breath as he rounded the corner, and when he reached Nick, the look on his face was one of grim satisfaction. 'See?' he murmured. 'Not even Grey is omnipotent.'

But Nick couldn't help noticing that he too kept his voice down to a whisper, as if nervous that the shopkeeper might overhear. No matter how safe they were supposed to be, Nick's gut wasn't relaxing any time soon. Grey was far too powerful to ever be written off.

Katie also skirted round the shopkeeper warily. 'What would happen if I touched him?' she asked.

'*Don't,*' Nick and Cavanagh said together.

She joined them at the entrance to the corridor, smoothing out her clothes in a nervous gesture. 'OK. Where do we go from here?'

'Deeper in.' Nick turned in the direction of the stairs. He moved more cautiously this time, afraid of hitting the top step before he realized it, and Katie cursed as she almost tripped over him.

'God, doesn't this place have any *lights?*'

'It does, but I don't know how to turn them on.' For all that the outer shop seemed to be lit by ordinary bulbs, it now occurred to Nick that he'd never actually seen any switches around to control them. Somehow he couldn't quite imagine that Mr Grey paid an electricity bill. 'Careful. Stairs coming up.'

He eased his way down them until his shoes bumped against the door at the bottom. He could hear and feel Cavanagh breathing close behind him.

'There's a ward here,' Cavanagh said tensely. 'A strong one. He's placed an enchantment to keep intruders out. Or do worse things . . .'

'Yeah.' Nick groped his hands over the surface of the door, trying to map out the carved pattern in his mind. He placed his palm over what he thought was the eye.

Energy pulsed through him and he shuddered with revulsion – for a moment he was back in Henry Jenkins's living room, feeling the bracelet pull and pull as it sucked the life out of the man, leaving behind an ugly, bloated corpse . . .

'Nick?' Katie's anxious nudge brought him back to the present.

'Yeah,' he said, his voice sounding scratchy and thin in the darkness. 'Um . . . I think that should have opened it.'

He gave the door a cautious push.

Unlike the rest of the shop, the underground chamber was lit. The unnatural glow cast deep shadows that flickered round the edges of the room, creating the illusion of motion at the corners of his eyes. It was like stepping into some vast subterranean treasure vault; only here, the treasure wasn't gold and jewels, but simple things of sentimental value. Rooting through it all seemed like robbing a mass grave.

Katie swore and swallowed, and Cavanagh said something under his breath in a language that Nick didn't know.

'The master orb's in here?' Katie asked.

'Somewhere. Maybe,' Nick said.

For a moment they all stood, silenced, aware of the vast task ahead of them – and the desperately limited time they had to complete it in.

XIX

'Where do we *start*?' Katie said, shaking her head hopelessly.

'At the very beginning.' Cavanagh stepped forward. 'The orb was Grey's first treasure, and his greatest. It won't be jammed in on a shelf just anywhere.'

'Can't you sense it?' she asked him. 'You said you could feel the power from those other orbs.'

He shook his head. 'Not behind Grey's wards. The master orb gives off so much power that any practitioner would be well aware of its presence if Grey didn't take steps to keep it hidden. I'm

237

effectively blind down here.' He turned to look at Nick. 'But you're not, Nick – do you feel anything?'

Feeling stupid, Nick closed his eyes and slowly moved his right arm from side to side. He was conscious of a throbbing from the bracelet, but it was hard to figure out if it was stronger in any one direction.

'I . . . really don't know,' he said, with a helpless shrug. 'It's like it's everywhere.'

Katie took a deep breath. 'OK then,' she said, with forced brightness. 'I guess we're splitting up. First one to find something, shout.'

They set off among the maze of shelves. As soon as the others were out of sight, Nick's heart started beating double time. For all Cavanagh's assurances, he was convinced Mr Grey was going to appear at any moment. He whirled round at every sound and flicker of movement, real or imagined. There was more breeze than there ought to be in a stone vault underground, and it licked at the back of his neck like a person's irregular breathing.

It was creepy as hell down there. He passed an entire section of shelves devoted to dolls and cuddly toys. Their dead, glassy eyes seemed to follow his movements, reminding him uncomfortably of Henry Jenkins's clouded stare.

Another shelf held a jumble of assorted weaponry: knives, antique swords, a crossbow, even rusted guns. Nick edged past that uneasily, trying not to wonder what they'd represented for their owners when they'd been traded in.

The room was a mix of over-intimate and meaningless, like seeing the debris left by a hurricane that had torn open people's homes and strewn their private belongings up and down the street. Every object here had a story attached, but they'd been ripped from the people who knew that history and now they were just old junk. Nick passed walls of photographs, framed and unframed, every person and event unfamiliar to him. Had the people in them forgotten too, traded memories and relationships away in return for whatever reward they believed to be so important?

He hustled on, beginning to feel dizzy. Everything seemed to leap out at him at once, every object demanding that he note its presence, study it, try to figure out its meaning . . . The maze of shelves seemed endless, and he began to feel like he could search for ever and never find what he was looking for – or the way back to the surface. He would wander this labyrinth until he died of starvation, and Grey would discover his desiccated corpse . . .

A jarring noise startled the life out of him. It took a second burst for him to realize what it was. His mobile phone was ringing.

Nick slowly drew it out of his pocket, unnerved and almost bewildered at the intrusion of the outer world. He gazed at the display, surprised to have even a single flickering bar of reception down here. The number was not one he recognized, and he raised it to his ear with trepidation in his gut. 'Hello?'

'Nick?' His name came through amid a crackle of static.

'Hello?' Nick repeated.

'Nick, it's Tariq.'

'Tariq?' he said in disbelief. 'How'd you get my number?'

The answer faded in and out as he moved past the shelves. 'Called . . . Spencers in town . . . got your dad. Listen . . . sent me that note?'

'I can barely hear you,' Nick said, trying to shout and whisper at the same time. He eyed the shadows nervously. 'Look, I'm sorry, I'm going to have to call you back. This is not exactly—'

'Nick . . . important. Whatever . . . don't . . . Cavanagh . . .'

'What?' Nick came to a halt and leaned this way and that in search of clearer reception.

'. . . hear me? I don't . . . got his . . .' As Nick raised the phone up higher, Tariq's voice suddenly came through sharper and louder, '. . . you do, do *not* trust Cavanagh.'

Nick's stomach dropped. 'Whoa, whoa. Hang on. Can you repeat that?' he said plaintively.

'Nick, you do not want to get involved with Alfred Cavanagh. The bloke is seriously bad news. Are you getting this?'

'Yeah,' he said dazedly. 'Um, what . . . ?'

'I know people who've had dealings with him before. He's part of some kind of . . .' The words dissolved into static again.

'He's part of *what*?' Nick strained to make out words.

'Cult. Cult. He's part of a cult. Real crazies. He sets himself up like . . . trying to help people, but he's only out to get revenge on Grey.'

'He says he can dissolve all the bargains,' Nick said, panic rising in his chest. Tariq had to be wrong. He'd put his trust in Cavanagh and it was too late to withdraw that trust now. It had to be a misunderstanding.

Tariq's deep huff of breath was audible even over the bad line. 'Yeah, well. I thought he could help me out with mine. Turns out his idea of a solution was to try and kill my sister.'

'He *what?*'

'He tried to *kill* my *sister.*' Tariq articulated the words so clearly there was no room for mistake. 'To reverse the bargain on Grey, see? I'm paying to keep her alive. If she dies, then Grey hasn't kept up his end of the bargain and he gets the backlash.'

Nick let out a sick sound. 'No. You must have – no . . .' he said feebly.

'I've heard stories, Nick,' Tariq continued. 'This cult that he belongs to – they *invented* the crystal ball things that Grey has. They used to *feed* people to them. Cavanagh may want to take down Grey, but that doesn't mean he cares about saving anybody. We're all just sacrifices to be thrown on the funeral pyre.'

'You're wrong,' Nick said, stomach tight.

'I'm not,' Tariq answered. 'Just take my advice, and stay away from Cavanagh.'

'Yeah – it's a little late for that!' Nick said, but he was talking to himself. He'd started moving again, and the reception fuzzed into nothing. He jabbed the phone off without saying goodbye and thrust it back in his pocket.

He had to find Katie. If Tariq's warning was accurate, then they were in a world of trouble. Their best bet might well be to flee while Cavanagh was still wandering the maze of shelves. If he could just get to Katie first . . .

'Nick!' The sharp yell stopped his heart, and it wasn't until Katie called again that he realized the tone was excitement, not terror. 'I think I've found it!'

The master orb. Nick's blood turned to ice. All of a sudden he wasn't sure that finding it was a good thing. And if he'd clearly heard that yell, then Cavanagh had too.

He ran towards her voice.

It was nearly impossible to progress through the labyrinth of shelves. He hit dead ends and unexpected U-turns, travelling half a dozen paces out of his way for every small step forward. He swiped one shelf unit with the bag slung over his shoulder, and winced as a snowstorm of papers fluttered to the ground. His heart pounded in the base of his throat at the thought of what might happen if Cavanagh got there before him.

Katie didn't call again, but he could feel where he needed to go from the waves of energy that pulsed out from the bracelet. They were growing stronger with every step he took. The master orb was definitely here.

As Nick rounded a final corner, fireworks went off behind his eyes. He staggered and almost fell, and Katie grabbed his arm.

'Nick? Nicky, are you OK? You look like you're going to puke.'

It was hard to focus on her as she peered at him. He couldn't tell if the lighting had changed or it was just his eyes. 'No. Yeah, I'm fine.' He forced the words out through teeth that were vibrating in sympathy with the bracelet. It was like standing on the edge of the platform as a high-speed train rattled by. 'What?'

'Look!' She dragged him towards an alcove in the wall. At first it seemed to be empty, but then he saw that both floor and ceiling were carved with a depiction of the eye and star symbol. Invisible energy crackled between the two symbols like a lightning bolt that had somehow been trapped and anchored. 'I wasn't sure if I should step in, but—'

'No,' he said hoarsely. Couldn't she *feel* it? She would have been fried to a crisp. 'That would have been . . . a pretty bad idea.'

'You think it's another door or something?'

'Or something,' Nick agreed tightly. He could barely think through the maelstrom in his head. The bracelet was pulling him along like a magnet. It was impossible to resist.

He stepped forward onto the carved stone of the alcove.

Energy flowed over him like a static shower. Every hair on his body stood up, and his skin burst instantly into goose flesh. His clothes crackled and stiffened, and the air he was breathing smelled burned. Sparks jumped from every piece of metal on his clothing. He raised his hands above his head, instinctively trying to shield himself from the flow. He felt the bracelet fill up with charge and start to overflow.

And then the world warped.

Not for a flickering instant like it did when he made a collection, but slowly. The clear lines of the shelves and flagstones wavered and became indistinct before blurring entirely. The light, the sound of his breathing, the solid stone beneath his feet: everything faded away, until Nick was drifting in absolute blankness. He felt nothing, thought nothing; it was as though he didn't have a body or a mind to feel or think with. He had no way to know if he hung there for less than a second or for a hundred million years.

And then the nothingness contracted in on itself, shrinking rapidly down until it was only the size of a house, a room . . . smaller. Until it was a black globe of emptiness hanging in front of his chest.

He reached out and took hold of the master orb.

It was the size of a football and made of thick, dark glass that was almost too dense to see through. It was etched all over with alien shapes and squiggles, though the surface felt smooth to the touch. Nick couldn't tell if it was warm or cold; his hands had gone utterly numb from the contact. It seemed at once far too light for its size and so heavy that he shouldn't be able to hold it.

And it whispered. Dark voices murmured at the back of his mind, not true words but half-formed feelings and sensations. Pleading, commanding, cajoling, seducing; wanting, wanting, wanting . . .

He backed out of the alcove slowly, feeling like he was holding a nuclear bomb.

'The sacred orb – at last, it's back in our hands.' Cavanagh's awed voice came out of nowhere, and Nick spun round, clutching the orb to his chest.

'Jesus!' Where the hell had he appeared from?

'What was all that, Nick? You've been in there for, like, five minutes,' Katie said.

'Yes. There's very little time left,' Cavanagh said. 'Give me the orb quickly. I have to cleanse it of Grey's corrupting influence.'

Instead of handing it over, Nick took a wary step away from him. 'Er . . . cleanse it how exactly?'

Cavanagh's face flickered with annoyance that he

quickly smoothed over. 'By breaking the bargains, as we discussed.'

Nick took another step back. 'Yeah, um, just out of curiosity' – he waved a hand to encompass all the shelves – 'what happens to all these people when their bargains . . . break?'

'They'll be released,' Cavanagh said, dark eyebrows lowering in a fierce frown.

Nick nodded slowly, still watching him for any sudden movement. 'Yeah, OK, but . . . released as in set free and given all their stuff back, or released as in . . . dead?'

'Nick . . . ?' Katie said slowly, edging away from both of them. 'What the hell are you on about?'

Nick was rather more interested in Cavanagh's non-reaction. *Too much* of a non-reaction.

'Katie, this thing is *not* a holy artefact,' he said. 'This thing *eats souls*. It wants to be *fed*.' He could feel the hunger coming off it in waves. He held Cavanagh's gaze. 'So considering you're a member of the same cult that made it, I've just got to wonder what'll *really* happen when you release all those deals at once. And what you're going to do with it afterwards.'

'This is ridiculous,' Cavanagh said.

And then made an abrupt lunge for the orb.

Nick barely jerked backwards in time, and he smacked his head on a shelf as he did so. A box of army medals skidded off and scattered over the stones.

'Well, that wasn't at all suspicious,' Katie said through a grimace, stepping sideways to join Nick.

Cavanagh's face had gone white with mounting anger. 'We have no *time*! Grey could be set free from the spell at any second. You have to give me the orb! I told you, I can help you!'

'Yeah, you told me,' Nick said. 'But I don't see what that proves. You see, Tariq Khalil just called me. He told me what your idea of help really involves.'

Cavanagh scowled, but Katie turned round to stare at Nick. 'Tariq just called you? As in, while we were inside the shop?'

'Er, Katie, not really important right now,' he said, still backing away from Cavanagh.

'Yes, important!' she said wildly. 'Nick, there's *no way* he should have been able to call you. We're supposed to be inside the bubble! Out of step with the rest of the world. If a phone call got through . . .'

Cavanagh's illusion spell. Nick realized with a sick chill that the greyed-out world around them had slipped back into full colour without him even noticing. They were no longer protected by Cavanagh's magic.

They were no longer shielded from Grey.

'Oh, very clever.' The shopkeeper stepped forward out of the shadows, giving a slow, sarcastic hand clap. 'Unfortunately, that's the only spark of intelligence that's been shown here tonight.' He turned his dark gaze towards Nick. 'Mr Spencer, I believe I told you the last time we met that you were not to come down here again.'

In the sudden silence, the click of Grey's heels was loud on the flagstones. He came forward to stand between Nick and Katie, and Cavanagh, still perfectly poised and utterly calm. He no longer looked small: the gravity of the room seemed to wrap itself around him, as if he was somehow more solid, more *real* than anything else.

The orb in Nick's hands thrummed like a welcoming purr.

Grey didn't stride forward to seize it, but simply turned his unblinking gaze on Nick. 'You would be advised to put that back where it belongs. Now, please.'

His eyes were black from edge to edge, the whites no longer evident. In their depths, Nick saw the same hungry nothingness he'd perceived inside the master orb. A great, sucking void that only wanted to consume and keep consuming.

Was Grey even human? Had he ever been? Nick didn't know if the malevolent force at the heart of the orb had found a kindred spirit in the shopkeeper, or simply taken him over so utterly that there was no longer any humanity left.

He only knew that he couldn't put the orb back in Grey's hands, no matter what.

Unfortunately, his only alternative wasn't looking a whole lot better.

Cavanagh stepped forward, practically vibrating with anger. 'Where it *belongs* is in the hands of the order.'

Grey raised one eyebrow. 'Ah, Brother Cavanagh. So you've elected to make your move at last. Your order never was one to learn from centuries of experience. I'm amazed you aren't fully extinct yet.'

'We will rise again, stronger than ever.' The light of fanaticism was in Cavanagh's eyes. 'All the world will come to know the truth. We will cleanse the Earth of the unworthy, and nothing will be left of your worthless little empire but dust and memory.' He clutched hold of the pendant around his neck.

Katie snaked out a hand and grabbed Nick's arm. 'OK, am I the only one here who doesn't like option A *or* B?' she said in an urgent whisper.

'No,' he replied faintly. The air was practically crackling between the two men as they eyed each other. Cavanagh was as tense and twitchy as a cat on the prowl, Grey, preternaturally still. Whichever one came out on top, Nick didn't want to be around to present them with the prize. 'Let's get out of here.'

They both turned and started to run – only to come to a windmilling halt as a set of shelves swung out sideways to cut off their path.

'I don't recall giving you permission to leave, Mr Spencer,' Grey said from behind them. 'The orb. Replace it. Now.'

Nick's chest tightened in panic, but Katie just barged forward into the shelves. The impact set them rocking, and her second push sent the unit right over in a violent cascade of trophies and ornaments. Nick scrambled over the debris with her, cringing guiltily as glass and wood crunched underfoot. He hugged the orb against his stomach as he ran, trying to ignore the numbing cold that radiated from it.

'This way!' Katie dragged him down another avenue. 'If we can just get back to the door—'

The shelves to either side of them spun away as if ripped out of place by a whirlwind. The ones beyond them followed, and Nick dropped to his knees, protecting the orb with his body as the chain reaction swept round the chamber. Shelf after shelf was ripped from its position and slammed against the walls with shattering force. A snowstorm of papers and photographs fluttered in their wake, and the room became a cacophony of smashing and crashing like some horrific traffic pile-up.

It went on for ever, and for ever, and for ever . . .

And then finally it stopped.

In the silence, Nick slowly raised his head. He was crouching in the middle of what could have been a bomb site. The labyrinth was gone. The wooden shelves that had comprised it now lay shattered along the outer walls of the huge chamber, their contents strewn over the ground in front of them. Drifts of papers almost buried the stone floor, some still raining down out of the sky like slow confetti.

A shaking Katie grasped Nick's elbow to pull herself up. Across from them, Cavanagh was slowly getting to *his* feet, his long hair in chaotic disarray. He patted a hand against his chest to be sure the crystal pendant was still there.

Only Grey seemed untouched by the storm. He stood, feet placed squarely apart, in the midst of the devastation. There was a neat circle in the debris around him – none of it had even touched him. His double-breasted suit was still as crisp and neat as if it had just been freshly ironed, and not a hair or thread looked out of place.

'Now,' he said, in the same tone of voice. 'Back to the matter of the orb.'

'Don't give it to him, Nick!' Cavanagh said, lurching forward. 'The orb belongs with the order. If you put it back in his hands, you're condemning all those people to slavery. You're going back to exactly what you tried to escape from.'

And the horrible thing was, that was true. Nick's

eyes prickled as the image of Mr Jenkins's corpse flashed through his mind. If he surrendered now, he was going back. To more collections. More death and more stolen dreams. Even if, by some ridiculously small chance, Grey released him from his bargain and he was free to go, the collections would still go on.

He stepped back, shaking his head. 'I'm not going to give it back.'

Grey lowered his eyebrows. 'Make no mistake, Mr Spencer, you are not the one who gets to make that choice. Replace the orb before I have to come and take it.' The shadows in the corners of the room swirled dangerously.

'Give it to me, Nick.' Cavanagh stepped forward, hands outstretched. 'I can protect you from him.'

Maybe it was even true . . . but that didn't make it right. If Cavanagh had the orb, he would use it to restore the order who had made it – at the expense of those whose souls were deemed 'unworthy'. But what did that mean? Murderers? Thieves? People who didn't pray four times a day? What percentage of the human race would Cavanagh decide didn't make the cut? Somehow Nick couldn't see a religion that had produced the orb preaching tolerance and second chances.

So what the hell was he supposed to do? Sweat poured down his forehead and trickled down his back, and the orb rattled dangerously in his hands. If he gave it back to Grey, he was perpetuating the chain of theft and slavery. If he gave it to Cavanagh, he was opening the way for a cult with the means to destroy anyone who didn't convert.

How could anybody make that decision? And how had it ever come to be laid on *his* shoulders?

Nick glanced over at Katie's drawn face, but he knew she couldn't help him on this one. It was his choice, and his alone. The fate of thousands was quite literally in his hands.

He looked down at the master orb. A voice in the back of his head whispered that he should run with it, steal it, learn how to use it. He could be as powerful as Grey. Build a much better world than the one Cavanagh dreamed of.

'Come on, Mr Spencer.' Grey's terse voice broke into his thoughts. 'You know there's only one way this can possibly end.'

'Yeah. There is.' Nick raised his head, and held the master orb out before him.

And then threw it down on the flagstones with all his strength.

It struck the floor with a dull clink instead of a smash, and Nick just had time to think, *Shit, it bounced . . .*

. . . before the world exploded.

The spot where the orb had landed became a bright maelstrom of energy, a brain-melting mess of colours and alien shapes. Bolts of multicoloured lightning lashed out from it like tentacles, striking the debris of Grey's trophy collection with sparks and crackling snaps. Nick threw himself to the ground as one passed within millimetres of his head.

'Nick!' Somehow, through the chaos, Katie managed to grab for his hand. 'What the hell is happening?'

'I don't know!' He'd hoped that smashing the orb would just *break* it, make it impossible for either of the men to take it, but he hadn't counted on setting off this kind of magical explosion. As they scrambled back, away from the heart of the energy storm, Nick saw Cavanagh moving towards it. His hair was whipping wildly around his head as he yanked the pendant off and held it out in front of him.

'The power of the sacred orb is unleashed!' he said, a note of hoarse triumph in his voice. 'Only the worthy will be spared!'

And he ran forward, into the blaze of light.

For a second it looked like he would truly be untouched by it – and then the energy seemed to *leap* at him, sparking over his skin. For a heartbeat he was there, the outline of a man wrapped up in threads of lightning . . . and then the threads unravelled, leaving nothing behind but an afterimage.

'Jesus!' Katie squeezed Nick's fingers hard enough to crack the bones.

'We've got to get out of here!' Nick looked wildly for the door.

That was when he saw Mr Grey. The shopkeeper's back was arched, his head thrown back, and he was at the centre of a halo of energy like the one around the broken orb. Nick couldn't tell if Grey was spasming in agony or exerting every bit of his power to protect himself from the blast.

He only knew that he didn't want to stick around to find out the result.

'Come on!' Holding on tight to Katie's hand, he stumbled across the room to the door they'd come in by. Sparks from a bolt of energy bit into his calf and he yelled out, his leg suddenly dead. He might have fallen if Katie hadn't kept on dragging him towards the stairs.

'Keep going!' she yelled as he went sprawling on the bottom step.

'No, wait!' Nick rolled over to look back through the doorway. The light show within had grown so unimaginably bright that he couldn't tell if Grey was even *in* there any more, never mind if he was alive or not.

He just hoped that the man's protective wards would survive beyond his death. Cavanagh had said the chamber was shielded so that the master orb was undetectable from outside. So maybe, if Nick could just seal the door shut . . .

He lurched to his feet and yanked the door towards him. As it clicked shut, he placed his right hand over the carving of the closed eye, and focused all his mental resources into one command. 'Seal!'

As he did so, he felt the impact of something striking the back of the door. Coloured lightning burst round the edges of it, rippling over the lines of the carved symbol . . . and surging into the bracelet around his wrist.

He screamed.

It felt like the flesh was melting off his bones. It was impossible to pull his hand back from the door; all the muscles had contracted, turning his grip into a suction seal, and his whole body was spasming uncontrollably. Electricity crawled over the lines of the bracelet and into his skin in a white-hot blaze of agony.

And then there was a small, soft click.

As the last of the lightning faded like a dying spark of static, the metal bracelet popped apart and slithered off his wrist. Nick sank to the ground, cradling his arm.

'Nick!' Katie swore and scrambled towards him. 'You all right?'

Nick had to take a moment to think about it. 'Er, yeah.' He found himself laughing helplessly for no particular reason. 'Yeah, I think so.' He clenched his right hand into a fist and opened it up again. 'Everything's still attached, anyway.'

He accepted a hand up from Katie, bracing himself against the door. It didn't swing open when he leaned his weight against it, and no noise or light spilled through from the room beyond. In the aftermath, the stairway seemed very dark and still. Either the energy storm was over, or he'd sealed it in successfully.

He wasn't about to open the door to find out which.

Nick took a slow, deep breath. He pushed his hair back off his face and patted himself down, half surprised to find he'd somehow held onto his school bag. He hadn't even had the time to think of tossing it away in all the chaos. 'OK. *Now* we should get out of here,' he said.

As he probed around in the dark for the bottom step, his foot brushed against the fallen bracelet. He kicked it away violently; he wasn't crazy enough to try and pick it up by hand. Maybe whatever magic had controlled it was irrevocably broken – but he wasn't about to take that chance.

They stumbled up the stairs and along the corridor. Nick didn't realize that they'd reached the orb room until he groped for more wall and found wood and cool glass.

'Why is it so bloody dark in here?' Katie muttered beside him.

'All the orbs have stopped glowing,' Nick said in wonder. 'They're empty.'

Mr Grey's unholy merchandise was gone. In smashing the master orb, he'd shattered whatever magic kept the things Grey bought and sold inside the smaller orbs.

He'd just put Bargains out of business.

'So what do you think happened to the stuff that was in them?' Katie asked as they made their way towards the outer door. 'I mean, did everybody get back the things they traded, or is it all just gone?'

'I don't know,' Nick said, then faltered for a moment. 'But there *is* a way I can find out,' he realized.

He started to run.

'You what?' Katie stumbled into a startled jog to keep up with him.

'Come on!' With a new burst of energy cutting through his weariness, Nick raced down the corridor and blasted through the door. He dashed along the darkened alleyway towards the lights of the town centre.

'Slow down, I'm knackered!' Katie protested. 'What's the hurry?'

Nick stopped in the alley mouth and ripped his school bag off his shoulder. He scrabbled frantically at the buckles and dragged out a random exercise book and a pencil.

'What should I draw?' he asked breathlessly.

There was a brief pause. 'I don't know why you're looking at me like you're expecting my brain to work,' Katie said wryly.

Nick's own imagination felt similarly dead, but he touched the pencil to paper anyway and sketched the first things that came into his head. A cube, a smiley face, a cartoon cat; none of it technically demanding – all of it appearing on the paper exactly as he pictured it in his head.

He threw the pencil up in the air, and didn't much care when he failed to catch it. 'I can draw!'

'Awesome!' Katie hugged him, and for a moment he just basked in relief so deep it made his knees weak.

All too soon, reality crept back in. Nick shot an uneasy glance back down the alley. There was no outward physical sign of the explosion they'd unleashed underground.

'You think Mr Grey could have survived that?' he asked.

Katie could only shrug. 'God knows. If anything Cavanagh said was true, then he shouldn't have been alive in the first place. You did just blow up the power source he was living on.'

'Yeah.' But Nick bit his lip uncertainly. Grey must have had some power of his own to have stolen the orb from the monks in the first place. And how many centuries had he had to come up with ways to protect himself if the worst happened? 'I suppose.'

'Anyway,' – Katie sucked in a big breath – 'whatever. It's not your problem any more. Let's go home.' She paused and frowned, looking at the deserted town. 'What the hell time is it, anyway?'

'I don't know.' Nick checked his watch, and found it flashing zeroes. 'Either it's exactly midnight, or my watch has stopped.'

'Want to crash in my garage?' Katie offered.

The idea was quite tempting, but he knew that if his parents *had* realized he was missing by now, he was better off facing them tonight than letting them worry until the morning.

'No,' he said, with a part-sigh, part-yawn. 'I guess I'd better go home.'

Nick went to his dad's, having told his mother that was where he was going hours and hours and hours ago. Any hopes of slipping in unnoticed were dashed when he saw the front window was still lit up. He resisted the urge to turn round and leave, and found the right key on his key ring.

He expected to be met by his dad and Julie, but he got a surprise. As he walked into the front hall, his mother and father came out to greet him.

'Hi,' he said stupidly after a moment, unable to think of much else.

'Nick,' his dad said flatly. He rubbed his beard, somehow managing to look tense *and* relieved at the same time.

'Got lost along the way, did you?' his mum said more lightly, but her eyebrows were furrowed.

Nick should have felt bad about worrying them, but he honestly wasn't sure he had the energy. 'I went for a walk,' he said, running a hand over his face. Now that the adrenaline rush of the confrontation with Grey was over, it was increasingly hard to stay upright.

'For hours? At this time of night?' his father demanded.

Nick's mum laid a cautioning hand on his arm. 'Will.'

'Er, yeah, um . . . I needed to clear my head,' Nick said. It was disconcerting facing both his parents together like this.

'What the hell is going on *in* your head?' his father roared. 'We had no idea where you were! I had some boy call up asking me for your mobile number, and it was only when I checked in with your mother that we even found out you were missing! And when I tried to get you, your phone was spitting out all kinds of error messages – we thought you'd been mugged!'

Nick thought of Cavanagh's spell, and the way his watch had been flashing when they left the shop. 'Oh, yeah. Er, I think something's gone funny with the battery. Sorry,' he said lamely.

That was enough to make his dad explode. 'Sorry! For God's *sake*, Nick—'

'Do you want to wake Kyle up?' his mother snapped. 'I thought we agreed we were going to handle this *calmly*?'

'*You* agreed,' his dad said caustically. 'I don't recall getting much of a say in the matter.' But there was a wry twist to his mouth, and the familiar bickering actually seemed to calm him down.

'And *this* is why.' His mum turned back and released her own tension in a slow breath. 'Nick . . . why did you lie to us?' she asked softly.

Nick shrugged uncomfortably, looking down at the carpet. 'I just . . . needed some space, I guess. I've been a bit . . . stressed lately.' To put it mildly. He scratched at the band of skin where the bracelet had until recently rested.

His mum sighed and leaned back against the wall. 'Is this our fault?' she asked.

'No!' he blurted out. 'I mean, it's just . . .'

'Because I know we bounce you about a lot, trying to keep you involved in everything—'

'I don't mind!' he insisted quickly.

His father sighed too. 'Look, Nick. I know you've got a lot on your plate right now . . .'

'I'm fine,' he said, starting to feel a little teary despite himself. He was well past the end of his emotional endurance, and this kind of apologetic concern was harder to weather than anger. It wasn't as if any of this was actually his parents' fault.

His dad leaned forward a little, trying to meet Nick's downturned gaze. 'You've got to tell us if we're putting too much pressure on you. We're not going to be cross if you don't spend every waking minute with your family. You're sixteen now. You've got your own life to be getting on with. You don't have to run yourself into the ground trying to please everybody.'

'It's not you,' Nick said, looking up. 'Really. It's just . . . everything.' He shook his head helplessly. 'It – it's been a *really* bad week.'

And maybe it was obvious that he was on the verge of tears, because his mum stepped forward and gave him a hug. 'Look, sugar. The important thing is that you're safe, OK?' she said. 'We can worry about everything else tomorrow. Now, at some point we're going to sit down and have a long talk about all this, but I think right now the best thing is that you just go to bed. Yeah?'

Nick sniffed. 'Yeah.'

'Good.' She kissed his cheek and let him go.

Surprisingly, his dad reached out and squeezed his shoulder too. 'Get some sleep,' he echoed. 'Don't worry about school in the morning, OK? I'll call in to tell them you're sick. And we'll talk some more when I get in tomorrow night.'

'OK.' Nick managed a watery smile. 'Thanks, Dad.'

'I'd better call James – tell him Nick's OK,' his mum said, straightening up. 'I'll speak to you on the phone sometime tomorrow, Will.'

'All right.' His dad gave her a weary nod. 'Goodnight, Miranda.'

Nick made his way through to the kitchen. Julie

was in there, quite obviously scratching around for ways to keep herself busy so she wouldn't interrupt anything. She gave him a tentative smile. 'Everything all right now?'

'Yeah.' He yawned. 'Sorry to keep you up.'

'Don't worry about it, love. You want some hot milk or something?' she offered.

'Er, no, it's OK.' He filled a glass of water from the tap and swigged it down. 'Think I'd better just go to bed.'

As he turned to leave the kitchen, he got a clear view through into the living room. The orb he'd given Julie for her birthday was still resting on the mantel-piece. Only now it was clear, blank glass, without the slightest hint of hazy smoke inside.

Nick made his way up the stairs, the simple effort suddenly seeming like a great feat of mountaineering. He had to haul himself up using the banister. As he reached the top, Kyle's door opened. His half-brother poked his head out, hair dishevelled. 'What's going on?'

'Nothing,' Nick said, yawning again. 'Go back to bed.'

Kyle squinted at him blearily. 'Is that your mum downstairs?' he persisted. 'Did something happen?'

'Nope,' Nick said. 'Everything is absolutely fine.'

And he realized that, for the first time in what felt like for ever, he was actually telling the truth.

He moved on to his own room, flopped face down on top of the covers without undressing, and fell straight into a deep sleep.

Epilogue

Nick slept most of the weekend away, and endured several more awkward conversations with his parents. Having convinced themselves they were smothering him with family commitments, they were now bending over backwards to give him more independence and control over his schedule. Despite feeling guilty, he was glad of the space. It was going to be hard to return to the mundane world of family dinners and football practices and caring about maths homework.

He had no physical scars to prove any of it had even happened, but phantom heat in his right arm made him twitch a dozen times a day. He wasn't sure if it was all in his head, or some kind of lingering nerve damage from the energy blast that had freed him from the bracelet. He often caught himself rubbing or scratching the skin when he was zoning out.

That seemed to happen to him a lot lately. He would be doing something completely ordinary, then a flash of light or a musty smell, or just any little thing, would kick him back to Henry Jenkins's front room or that final confrontation down in the underground warehouse. It sometimes took him a moment to realize that he wasn't physically *there* and force his way out of the panic attack.

He and Katie exchanged texts and phone calls over the weekend, but they didn't talk about what had happened. The memories of that night seemed somehow fragile, as if it would all unravel into crazy threads if they talked it over afterwards. Instead, Nick listened while Katie rambled about what had happened in school on Friday, and responded with stories of his conversations with his parents. It was a relief, honestly, to pretend to be thinking about something other than the shop.

On the Sunday, Nick finally called Tariq back. 'How's your sister?' he asked tentatively.

'She's fine . . . What happened, man? I was talking to you, then I lost the signal, and then ten minutes later my scars were gone! What's going on with the shop?'

'Cavanagh and Grey had a . . . sort of fight.' For some reason he felt awkward mentioning his own part in it. 'They both lost. I don't know if Grey's dead or what, but he lost control of all the bargains.'

Tariq sucked in a slow, rattling breath. 'So, what . . . we're all in the clear? For good?' he asked.

'I don't know,' Nick was forced to admit. 'I guess. I hope so.'

'Wow.'

'Yeah.' They both waited awkwardly for a moment, before realizing they didn't have anything more to say to each other. 'Um, anyway, I just thought you ought to know,' Nick said. 'So, er . . . bye, then.'

He saw Hannah Armstrong in the corridors at school a few times, but was always quick to duck away before she could spot him. He was pretty sure he didn't want to know how the severing of the bargain had worked out for her – whether her mother would be leaving now, and if she was relieved to have her piano talent back, or heartbroken that the deal she'd made had been taken away from her.

He could have damned as many people as he saved by shattering that orb. Surely at least some of the people who'd made deals with the shop had got something they wanted or needed out of it? How many lives had he ruined by wrenching those bargains away?

He tried not to think about it.

After almost a week, Nick finally worked up the courage to return to the alley where he'd found the shop. He wasn't sure how well his memory was steering him, and though he looked and looked, he couldn't spot the Bargains sign in the upper windows. Finally, after a slow and methodical search of every building, he found what he was sure was the shop door. It looked somehow more faded and weathered than it did in his recollections, as if time had decided to attack more aggressively in the days since he'd been there.

Nick pressed his hand against it, half expecting to

feel a pulse through his skin as he had when he was wearing the bracelet. But he felt nothing, and the door didn't open. Either it was stuck fast, or it was locked.

Bargains was closed.

He stood staring at the door for a long time before he turned and walked away.

Three weeks later, he was sitting in his college interview. Even though he'd seen for himself that his drawing skills had returned, Nick couldn't help but feel a shiver of nerves. What if, after all this, it still wasn't enough? What if he'd been fooling himself all along? What if he'd never had the skills to make it as a professional artist, and everything he'd done to get to this point was completely futile?

He couldn't read his interviewer's face at all. Her name was Annie Watkins, and she was a big, solid, grey-haired woman with a brisk, no-nonsense manner. From her steely mask as she pored over his precious portfolio, she could just as easily have been reading her insurance documents. Nick rubbed his right wrist nervously.

'Is this a recent work?' She suddenly turned the

folder to face him, and Nick couldn't help but flinch at the sight of the sketch that she'd picked out. He'd hesitated over including it – in fact, he really wished that he'd never drawn it at all – but it really *was* an excellent sketch. He'd captured the essence of his subject perfectly.

Entirely *too* perfectly. The sight of Mr Grey staring up at him, even in shades of pencil lead, was enough to put him off his stride completely.

'Oh, er, yes. It is, yeah,' he said stupidly.

Ms Watkins nodded to herself. 'It's very good. It's got a depth to it that some of your earlier work is lacking. Very evocative. And I like the title. *The Shopkeeper* – nice and enigmatic. This fellow looks like he could sell you just about anything, doesn't he?'

Nick endured her amused titter, and hoped she would blame his sickly return smile on interview nerves.

'Yes. There's some good work here.' She closed the portfolio and stood up. 'I'm very pleased to have met you, Nick, and I think you'll be a great addition to our class. You make sure you get the GCSEs you need, and there'll definitely be a place for you here in September.' She held out her hand to him.

Nick hesitated for a fraction longer than he should have before taking it. The gesture of shaking hands on an agreement was never going to seem entirely innocent to him again.

He left the office and looked around, trying to get his bearings. It was twenty to five, and there were enough students still wandering the halls to make him feel embarrassed about stopping to consult a wall map. He picked a corridor that looked like the right one and started down it.

As he did so, a glint of light caught the corner of his eye. His paranoid reflexes made him whip round, hunting for the source. It was the overhead light, reflecting off a ball one of the students had just tossed in the air.

A glass ball, full of silver smoke.

Almost hypnotized by the sight of it, Nick found that he was walking forward before he'd consciously decided to move.

A girl with dreadlocks was hanging on the arm of the boy who'd just tossed the orb. 'So where'd you get it from?' she was asking as Nick drew closer.

The boy jerked a thumb over his shoulder. 'This new shop. It's just opened up down the road.' He gave a huff of a laugh. 'I'm telling you, the shopkeeper was a *right* weirdo. He was asking me about that maths prize thing I won last year – God knows how he even knew about it. He even asked me to write an equation for him. I mean, seriously, what the *hell*? He must be some kind of crazy maths groupie.'

They both laughed. Neither of them noticed the blood draining from Nick's face as he eavesdropped.

'It's pretty,' the girl said, gesturing for the boy to give it to her. She held it up to admire it under the light. 'I might get my mum one. How much did you say it cost you?'

The boy's face crinkled up in a frown. 'You know, that's the *really* crazy thing. I tried to offer him money for it, and you know what he said?' He smirked and shook his head. 'He said I'd already given him more than enough.'